Luther and the Reformation: The Life-Springs of Our Liberties

Joseph A. Seiss

Contents

PREFACE. 7

LUTHER AND THE REFORMATION...8

THE FOUNDING OF PENNSYLVANIA. 73

    I. THE HISTORY AND THE MEN..73

    II. THE PRINCIPLES ENTHRONED. 91

LUTHER AND THE REFORMATION: THE LIFE-SPRINGS OF OUR LIBERTIES

BY

Joseph A. Seiss

PREFACE.

The first part of this book presents the studies of the Author in preparing a Memorial Oration delivered in the city of New York, November 10, 1883, on the four hundredth anniversary of the birth of Martin Luther. The second part presents his studies in a like preparation for certain Discourses delivered in the city of Philadelphia at the Bi-Centennial of the founding of the Commonwealth of Pennsylvania. There was no intention, in either case, to make a book, however small in size. But the utterances given on these occasions having been solicited for publication in permanent shape for common use, and the two parts being intimately related in the exhibition of the most vital springs of our religious and civil freedom, it has been concluded to print these studies entire and together in this form, in hope that the same may satisfy all such desires and serve to promote truth and righteousness.

Throughout the wide earth there has been an unexampled stir with regard to the life and work of the great Reformer, and these presentations may help to show it no wild craze, but a just and rational recognition of God's wondrous providence in the constitution of our modern world.

And to Him who was, and who is, and who is to come, the God of all history and grace, be the praise, the honor, and the glory, world without end!

THANKSGIVING DAY, 1883.

LUTHER AND THE REFORMATION.

A rare spectacle has been spreading itself before the face of heaven during these last months.

Millions of people, of many nations and languages, on both sides of the ocean, simultaneously engaged in celebrating the birth of a mere man, four hundred years after he was born, is an unwonted scene in our world.

Unprompted by any voice of authority, unconstrained by any command of power, we join in the wide-ranging demonstration.

In the happy freedom which has come to us among the fruits of that man's labors we bring our humble chaplet to grace the memory of one whose worth and services there is scarce capacity to tell.

HUMAN GREATNESS.

Some men are colossal. Their characters are so massive, and their position in history is so towering, that other men can hardly get high enough to take their measure. An overruling Providence so endows and places them that they affect the world, turn its course into new channels, impart to it a new spirit, and leave their impress on all the ages after them. Even humble individuals, without titles, crowns, or physical armaments, have wrought themselves into the very life of the race and built their memorials in the characteristics of epochs.

History tells of a certain Saul of Tarsus, a lone and friendless man, stripped of all earthly possessions, forced into battle with a universe of enthroned superstition, encompassed by perils which threatened every hour to dissolve him, who, pressing his way over mountains of difficulty and through seas of suffering, and dying a martyr to his cause, gave to Europe a living God and to the nations another and an everlasting King.

We likewise read of a certain Christopher Columbus, brooding in lowly retirement upon the structure of the physical universe, ridiculed, frowned on by the learned, repulsed by court after court, yet launching out into the unknown seas to find an undiscovered hemisphere, and opening the way for persecuted Liberty to cradle the grand empire of popular rule amid the golden hills of a new and independent continent.

And in this category stands the name of MARTIN LUTHER.

He was a poor, plain man, only a doctor of divinity, without place except as a teacher in a university, without power or authority except in the convictions and qualities of his own soul, and with no implements save his Bible, tongue, and pen; but with him the ages divided and human history took a new departure.

Two pre-eminent revolutions have passed over Europe since the beginning of the Christian era. The one struck the Rome and rule of emperors; the other struck the Rome and rule of popes. The one brought the Dark Ages; the other ended them. The one overwhelmed the dominion of the Caesars; the other humiliated a more than imperial dominion reared in Caesar's place. Alaric, Rhadagaisus, Genseric, and Attila were the chief instruments and embodiment of the first; *Martin Luther* was the chief instrument and embodiment of the second. The one wrought bloody desolation; the other brought blessed renovation, under which humanity has bloomed its happiest and its best.

THE PAPACY.

Since Phocas decreed the bishop of Rome the supreme head of the Church on earth there had grown up strange power which claimed to decide beyond appeal respecting everybody and everything--from affairs of empire to the burial of the dead, from the thoughts of men here to the estate of their souls hereafter--and to command the anathemas of God upon any who dared to question its authority. It held itself divinely ordained to give crowns and to take them away. Kings and potentates were its vassals, and nations had to defer to it and serve it, on pain of *interdicts* which smote whole realms with gloom and desolation, prostrated all the industries of life, locked up the very graveyards against decent sepulture, and consigned peoples and generations to an irresistible damnation. It was omnipresent and omnipotent in civilized Europe. Its clergy and orders swarmed in every place, all sworn to guard it at every point on peril of their souls, and themselves held sacred in person and retreat from all reach of law for any crime save lack of fealty to the great autocracy.[1] The money, the armies, the lands, the legislatures, the judges, the executives, the police, the schools, with the whole ecclesiastical administration, reaching even to the most private affairs of life, were under its control. And at its centre sat its absolute dictator, unanswerable and supreme, the alleged Vicar of God on earth, for whom to err was deemed impossible.

Think of a power which could force King Henry IV., the heir of a long line of emperors, to strip himself of every mark of his station, put on the linen dress of a penitent, walk barefooted through the winter's snow to the pope's castle at Canossa, and there to wait three days at its gates, unbefriended, unfed, and half perishing with cold and hunger, till all but the alleged Vicar of Jesus Christ were moved with pity for his miseries as he stood imploring the tardy clemency of Hildebrand, which was almost as humiliating in its bestowal as in its reservation.

Think of a power which could force the English king, Henry II., to walk three miles of a flinty road, with bare and bleeding feet, to Canterbury, to be flogged from one end of the church to the other by the beastly monks, and then forced to spend the whole night in supplications to the spirit of an obstinate, perjured, and defiant archbishop, whom four of his over-zealous knights, without his orders, had murdered, and whose inner garments, when he was stripped to receive his shroud, were found alive with vermin!

Think of a power which, in defiance of the sealed safe-conduct of the empire, could seize John Huss, one of the worthiest and most learned men of his time, and burn him alive in the presence of the emperor!

Think of a power which, by a single edict, caused the deliberate murder of more than fifty thousand men in the Netherlands alone!

Note:

[1] Many assumed the clerical character for no other reason than that it might screen them from the punishment which their actions deserved, and the monasteries were full of people who entered them to be secure against the consequences of their crimes and atrocities.--Rymer's *Foedera*, vol. xiii. p. 532.

EFFORTS AT REFORM.

To restrain and humble this gigantic power was the desideratum of ages. For two hundred years had men been laboring to curb and tame it. From theologians and universities, from kings and emperors, from provinces and synods, from general councils, and even the College of Cardinals--in every name of right, virtue, and religion--appeal after appeal and solemn effort after effort were made to reform the Roman court and free the world from the terrible oppression. Wars on wars were waged; provinces on provinces were deluged with blood; coalitions, bound by sacred oaths, were formed against the giant tyranny. And yet the hierarchy managed to maintain its assumptions and to overwhelm all remedial attempts. Whether made by individuals or secular powers, by councils or governments, the result was the same. The Pontificate still triumphed, with its claims unabridged, its dominion unbroken, its scandals uncured.

A general council sat at Constance to reform the clergy in head and members. It managed to rid itself of three popes between whom Christendom was divided, when the emperor moved that the work of reform proceed. But the cardinals said, How can the Church reform itself without a head? So they elected a pope who was to lead reform. Yet a day had hardly passed before they found themselves in a traitor's power, who reaffirmed all the acts of the iniquitous John XXIII., who had just been deposed for his crimes, and presently endowed him with a cardinal's hat!

When this pope, Martin V., died, the cardinals thought to remedy their previous mistake. They would secure their reforms before electing a pope. So they erected themselves into a standing senate, without which no future pope could act. And they each took solemn oath, before God and all angels, by St. Peter and all apostles, by the holy sacrament of Christ's body and blood, and by all the powers that be, if elected, to conform to these arrangements and to use all the rights and prerogatives of the sublime position to put in force the reforms conceded to be necessary.

But what are oaths and fore-pledges to candidates greedy for office? The tickets which elected the new pope had hardly been counted when he absolved himself from all previous obligations, disowned the senate of cardinals he had helped to erect, began his career with violence and robbery, plundered the cities and states of Italy, religiously violated all compacts but those which favored his absolute supremacy, brought to none effect the reform Council of Basle, deceived Germany with his specious and hollow concessions, averted the improvements he had sworn to make, and by his perfidy and cunning managed to retain in subordination to the old regime nearly the whole of that Christendom which he had outraged!

In spite of the efforts of centuries, this super-imperial power held by the throat a struggling world.

To break that gnarled and bony hand, which locked up everything in its grasp; to bring down the towering altitude of that olden tyranny, whose head was lifted to the clouds; to strike from the soul its clanking chains and set the suffering nations free; to champion the inborn rights of afflicted humanity, and conquer the ignorance and imposture which had governed for a thousand years,--constituted the work and office of the man the four hundredth anniversary of whose birth half the civilized world is celebrating to-day.

TIME OF THE REFORMATION.

It has been said that when this tonsured Augustinian came upon the stage almost any brave man might have brought about the impending changes. The Reformers before the Reformation, though vanquished, had indeed not lived in vain. The European peoples were outgrowing feudal vassalage, and moving toward nationalization and separation between the secular and ecclesiastical powers. Travel, exploration, and discovery had introduced new subjects of human interest and contemplation. Schools of law, medicine, and liberal education were being established and largely attended. The common mind was losing faith in the professions and teachings of the old hierarchy. Free inquiry was overturning the dominion of authority in matters of thought and opinion. The intellect of man was beginning to recover from the nightmare of centuries. A mightier power than the sword had sprung up in the art of printing. In a word, the world was gravid with a new era. But it was not so clear who would be able to bring it safely to the birth.

There were living at the time many eminent men who might be thought of for this office had it not been assigned to Luther. Reuchlin, Erasmus, Huetten, Sickingen, and others have been named, but the list might be extended, and yet no one be found endowed with the qualities to accomplish the work that was needed and that was accomplished.

FREDERICK THE WISE.

The Saxon Elector, Frederick the Wise, was the worthiest, most popular, and most influential ruler then in Europe. He could have been emperor in place of Charles V. had he consented to be. The history of the world since his time might have been greatly different had he yielded to the general desire. His principles, his attainments, his wisdom, and his spirit were everything to commend him. He founded the University of Wittenberg in hope that it would produce preachers who would leave off the cold subtleties of Scholasticism and the uncertainties of tradition, and give discourses that would possess the nerve and power of the Gospel of God. He sought out the best and most pious men for his advisers. He was the devoted friend of learning, truth, and virtue. By his prudence and foresight in Church and State he helped the Reformation more than any other man then in power. Had it not been for him perhaps Luther could not have succeeded. But it was not in the nature of things for the noble Elector to give us such a Reformation as that led by his humble subject. It is useless to speculate as to what the Reformation might have become in his hands; but it certainly could never have become what we rejoice to know it was, while the probabilities are that we would now be fighting the battles which Luther fought for us three and a half centuries ago.

REUCHLIN.

Reuchlin was a learned and able man, and deeply conscious of the need of reform. When the Greek Argyrophylos heard him read and explain Thucydides, he exclaimed, "Greece has retired beyond the Alps." He was the first Hebrew scholar of Germany, and served to restore the Hebrew Scriptures to the knowledge of the Church. He held that popes could err and be deceived. He had no faith in human abnegations for reconciliation with God. He saw no need for hierarchical mediations, and discredited the doctrine of Purgatory and masses for the dead. He bravely defended the cause of learning against the ignorant monks, whom he hated and held up to merciless ridicule. He was a brilliant and persuasive orator. He was an associate and counselor of kings. He gave Melanchthon to the Reformation, and did much to promote it. Luther recognized in him a great light, of vast service to the Gospel in Germany. But Reuchlin could never have accomplished the Reformation. The vital principles of it were not sufficiently rooted in him. He was a humanist, whose sympathies went with the republic of letters, not with the wants of the soul and the needs of the people. When he got into trouble he appealed to the pope. And though he lived to see Luther in agonizing conflict with the hierarchy of Rome, he refrained from making common cause with him, and died in connection with the unreformed Church, whose doctrines he had questioned and whose orders he had so unsparingly ridiculed.

ERASMUS OF ROTTERDAM.

Erasmus was a notable man, great in talent and of great service in preparing the way for the Reformation. He turned reviving learning to the study of the Word. He produced the first, and for a long time the only, critical edition of the New Testament in the original, to which he added a Latin translation and notes. He paraphrased the Epistle to the Romans--that great Epistle on which above all, the Reformation moved. Though once an inmate of a monastery, he abhorred the monks and exposed them with terrible severity. He had more friends, reputation, and influence than perhaps any other private man in Europe. And he was deep in the spirit of opposition to the scandalous condition of things in the Church. But he never could have given us the Reformation. He said all honest men sided with Luther, and as an honest man his place would have been by Luther's side; but he was too great a coward. "If I should join Luther," said he, "I could only perish with him, and I do not mean to run my neck into the halter. Let popes and emperors settle matters."--"Your Holiness says, Come to Rome; you might as well tell a crab to fly. If I write calmly against Luther, I shall be called lukewarm; if I write as he does, I shall stir up a hornet's nest.... Send for the best and wisest men in Christendom, and follow their advice."--"Reduce the dogmas necessary to be believed to the smallest possible number. On other points let every one believe as he likes. Having done this, quietly correct the abuses of which the world justly complains."

So wrote Erasmus to the pope and to the archbishop of Mayence. Such was his ideal of reformation--a thing as impossible to bring into practical effect as its realization would have been absurd. It is easy to tell a crab to fly, but will he do it? As well propose to convert infallibility with a fable of AEsop as to count on bringing regeneration to the hierarchy by such counsels.

The waters were too deep and the storms too fierce for the vacillating Erasmus. He did some excellent service in his way, but all his counsels and ideas failed, as they deserved. Once the idol of Europe, he died a defeated, crushed, and miserable man. "Hercules could not fight two monsters at once," said he, "while I, poor wretch! have lions, cerberuses, cancers, scorpions, every day at my sword's point.... There is no rest for me in my age, unless I join Luther; and that I cannot, for I cannot accept his doctrines. Sometimes I am stung with desire to avenge my wrongs; but my heart says, Will you in your spleen raise hand against your mother who begot you at the font? I cannot do it. Yet, because I bade monks remember their vows; because I told persons to leave off their wranglings and read the Bible; because I told popes and cardinals to look to the apostles and be more like them,--the theologians say I am their enemy."

Thus in sorrow and in clouds Erasmus passed away, as would the entire Reformation in his hands.

ULRIC VON HUeTTEN.

Ulric von Huetten, soldier and knight, equally distinguished in letters and in arms, and called the Demosthenes of Germany, was a zealous friend of reform. He had been in Rome, and sharpened his darts from what he there saw to hurl them with effect. All the powers of satire and ridicule he brought to bear upon the pillars of the Papacy. He helped to shake the edifice, and his plans and spirit might have served to pull it down had he been able to bring Europe to his mind; but it would only have been to bury society in its ruins.

ULRICH ZWINGLI.

Ulrich Zwingli is ranked among Reformers, and he was energetic in behalf of reform. But he fell a victim to his own mistakes, and with him would have perished the Reformation also had it depended upon him. Even had he lived, his radical and rationalistic spirit, his narrow and fiery patriotism, his shallow religious experience, and his eagerness to rest the cause of Reformation on civil authority and the sword, would have wrecked it with nine-tenths of the European peoples.

MELANCHTHON.

Philip Melanchthon was a better and a greater man, and did the Reformation a far superior service. Luther would have been much disabled without him, and Germany has awarded him the title of its "Preceptor." But no Reformation could have come if the fighting or directing of its battles had been left to him. Even with the great Luther ever by his side, he could hardly get loose from Rome and retain his wholeness, and when he was loose could hardly maintain his legs upon the ground that had been won.

CALVIN.

John Calvin was a man of great learning and ability. Marked has been his influence on the theology and government of a large portion of the Reformed churches. But the Reformation was twelve years old before he came into it. It had to exist already ere there could be a Calvin, while his repeated flights to avoid danger prove how inadequate his courage was for such unflinching duty as rendered Luther illustrious. He was a cold, hard, ascetic aristocrat at best, more cynical, stern, and tyrannical than brave. The organization for the Church and civil government which he gave to Geneva was quite too intolerant and inquisitorial for safe adoption in general or to endure the test of the true Gospel spirit. Under a regime which burnt Servetus for heresy, threw men into prison for reading novels, hung and beheaded children for improper behavior toward parents, whipped and banished people for singing songs, and dealt with others as public blasphemers if they said a word against the Reformers or failed to go to church, the cause of the Reformation could never have commanded acceptance by the nations, or have survived had it been received. The famous "Blue Laws" of the New England colonies have had to be given up as a scandal upon enlightened civilization; but they were largely transcribed from Calvin's code and counsels, including even the punishing of witches. For the last two hundred years the Calvinistic peoples have been reforming back from Calvin's rules and spirit, either to a better foundation for the perpetuation and honor of the Church or to a rationalistic skepticism which lets go all the distinctive elements of the genuine Christian Creed--the natural reaction from the hard and overstrained severity of a legalistic style of Christianity.

With all the great service Calvin has rendered to theological science and church discipline, there was an unnatural sombreness about him, which linked him rather with the Middle Ages and the hierarchical rule than with the glad, free spirit of a wholesome Christian life. At twenty-seven he had already drawn up a formula of doctrine and organization which he never changed and to which he ever held. There was no development either in his life or in his ideas. The evangelic elements of his system he found ready to his hand, as thought out by Luther and the German theologians. They did not originate or grow with him. And had the Reformation depended upon him it could never have become a success. So too with any others that might be named.

LUTHER THE CHOSEN INSTRUMENT.

We may not limit Providence. The work was to be done. Every interest of the world and of the kingdom of God demanded it. And if there had been no Luther at hand, some one else would have been raised up to serve in his place. But there ***was*** a Luther, and, as far as human insight can determine, he was the only man on earth competent to achieve the Reformation. And he it was who did achieve it.

Looked at in advance, perhaps no one would have thought of him for such an office. He was so humbly born, so lowly in station, so destitute of fortune, and withal so honest a Papist, that not the slightest tokens presented to mark him out as the chosen instrument to grapple with the magnitudinous tyranny by which Europe was enthralled.

But "God hath chosen the weak things of the world to confound the things that are mighty." Moses was the son of a slave. The founder of the Hebrew monarchy was a shepherd-boy. The Redeemer-King of the world was born in a stable and reared in the family of a village carpenter. And we need not wonder that the hero-prophet of the modern ages was the son of a poor toiler for his daily bread, and compelled to sing upon the street for alms to keep body and soul together while struggling for an education.

It has been the common order of Providence that the greatest lights and benefactors of the race, the men who rose the highest above the level of their kind and stood as beacons to the world, were not such as would have been thought of in advance for the mighty services which render their names immortal. And that the master spirit of the great Reformation was no exception all the more surely identifies that marvelous achievement as the work of an overruling God.

LUTHER'S ORIGIN.

Luther was a Saxon German--a German of the Germans--born of that blood out of which, with but few exceptions, have sprung the ruling powers of the West since the last of the old Roman emperors. He came out of the bosom of the freshest, strongest, and hardiest peoples then existing--the direct descendants of those wild Cimbrian and Teutonic tribes who, even in their heathenism, were the most virtuous, brave, and true of all the Gentiles.

Nor was he the offspring of enfeebled, gouty, aristocratic blood. He was the son of the sinewy and sturdy yeomanry. Though tradition reports one of his remote ancestors in something of imperial place among the chieftains of the semi-savage tribes from which he was descended, when the period of the Reformation came his family was in like condition with that of the house of David when the Christ was born. His father and grandfather and great-grandfather, he says himself, were true

Thuringian peasants.

LUTHER'S EARLY TRAINING.

In the early periods of the mediaeval Church her missionaries came to these fiery warriors of the North and followed the conquests of Charlemagne, to teach them that they had souls, that there is a living and all-knowing God at whose judgment-bar all must one day stand to give account, and that it would then be well with the believing, brave, honest, true, and good, and ill with cowards, profligates, and liars. It was a simple creed, but it took fast hold on the Germanic heart, to show itself in sturdy power in the long after years.

This creed, in unabated force, descended to Luther's parents, and lived and wrought in them as a controlling principle. They were also strict to render it the same in their children.

Hans Luther was a hard and stern disciplinarian, unsparing in the enforcement of every virtue.

Margaret Luther[2] was noted among her neighbors as a model woman, and was so earnest in her inculcations of right that she preferred to see her son bleed beneath the rod rather than that he should do a questionable thing even respecting so small a matter as a nut.

From his childhood Luther was thus trained and attempered to fear God, reverence truth and honesty, and hate hypocrisy and lies. Possibly his parents were severer with him than was necessary, but it was well for him, as the prospective prophet of a new era, to learn absolute obedience to those who were to him the representatives of that divine authority which he was to teach the world supremely to obey.

But no birth, or blood, or parental drilling, or any mere human culture, could give the qualities necessary to a successful Reformer. The Church had fallen into all manner of evils, because it had drifted away from the apostolic doctrine as to how a man shall be just with God; which is the all-conditioning question of all right religion. There could then be no cure for those evils except by the bringing of the Church back to that doctrine. But to do anything effectual toward such a recovery it was pre-eminently required that the Reformer himself should first be brought to an experimental knowledge of what was to be witnessed and taught.

On two different theatres, therefore, the Reformation had to be wrought out:

first, in the Reformer's own soul, and then on the field of the world outside of him.

Note:

[2] The maiden name of Margaret Luther, the mother of Martin, was ***Margaret Ziegler***. There has been a traditional belief that her name was Margaret Lindeman. The mistake originated in confounding Luther's grandmother, whose name was ***Lindeman***, with Luther's mother, whose name was ***Ziegler***. Prof. Julius Koestlin, in his ***Life of Luther***, after a thorough examination of original records and documents, gives this explanation.

WHAT THE REFORMATION WAS.

It is hard to take in the depth and magnitude of what is called The Great Reformation. It stands out in history like a range of Himalayan mountains, whose roots reach down into the heart of the world and whose summits pierce beyond the clouds.

To Bossuet and Voltaire it was a mere squabble of the monks; to others it was the cupidity of secular sovereigns and lay nobility grasping for the power, estates, and riches of the Church. Some treat of it as a simple reaction against religious scandals, with no great depths of principle or meaning except to illustrate the recuperative power of human society to cure itself of oppressive ills. Guizot describes it as "a vast effort of the human mind to achieve its freedom--a great endeavor to emancipate human reason." Lord Bacon takes it as the reawakening of antiquity and the recall of former times to reshape and fashion our own.

Whatever of truth some of these estimates may contain, they fall far short of a correct idea of what the Reformation was, or wherein lay the vital spring of that wondrous revolution. Its historic and philosophic centre was vastly deeper and more potent than either or all of these conceptions would make it. Many influences contributed to its accomplishment, but its inmost principle was unique. The real nerve of the Reformation was religious. Its life was something different from mere earthly interests, utilities, aims, or passions. ***Its seat was in the conscience.*** Its true spring was the soul, confronted by eternal judgment, trembling for its estate before divine Almightiness, and, on pain of banishment from every immortal good, forced to condition and dispose itself according to the clear revelations of God. It was not mere negation to an oppressive hierarchy, except as it was first positive and evangelic touching the direct and indefeasible relations and obligations of the soul to its

Maker. Only when the hierarchy claimed to qualify these direct relations and obligations, thrust itself between the soul and its Redeemer, and by eternal penalties sought to hold the conscience bound to human authorities and traditions, did the Reformation protest and take issue. Had the inalienable right and duty to obey God rather than man been conceded, the hierarchy, as such, might have remained, the same as monarchical government. But this the hierarchy negatived, condemned, and would by no means tolerate. Hence the mighty contest. And the heart, sum, and essence of the whole struggle was the maintenance and the working out into living fact of this direct obligation of the soul to God and the supreme authority of His clear and unadulterated word.

SPIRITUAL TRAINING.

How Luther came to these principles, and the fiery trials by which they were burnt into him as part of his inmost self, is one of the most vital chapters in the history.

His father had designed him for the law. To this end he had gone through the best schools of Germany, taken his master's degree, and was advancing in the particular studies relating to his intended profession, when a sudden change came over his life.

Religious in his temper and training, and educated in a creed which worked mainly on man's fears, without emphasizing the only basis of spiritual peace, he fell into great terrors of conscience. Several occurrences contributed to this: (1) He fell sick, and was likely to die. (2) He accidentally severed an artery, and came near bleeding to death. (3) A bosom friend of his was suddenly killed. All this made him think how it would be with him if called to stand before God in judgment, and filled him with alarm. Then (4) he was one day overtaken by a thunderstorm of unwonted violence. The terrific scene presented to his vivid fancy all the horrors of a mediaeval picture of the Last Day, and himself about to be plunged into eternal fire. Overwhelmed with terror, he cried to Heaven for help, and vowed, if spared, to devote himself to the salvation of his soul by becoming a monk. His father hated monkery, and he shared the feeling; but, if it would save him, why hesitate? What was a father's displeasure or the loss of all the favors of the world to his safety against a hopeless perdition?

Call it superstition, call it religious melancholy, call it morbid hallucination, it was a most serious matter to the young Luther, and out of it ultimately grew the Reformation. False ideas underlay the resolve, but it was profoundly sincere and according to the ideas of ages. It was wrong, but he could not correct the error until he had tested it. And thus, by what he took as the unmistakable call of God, he entered the cloister.

Never man went into a monastery with purer motives. Never a man went through the duties, drudgeries, and humiliations of the novitiate of convent-life with more unshrinking fidelity. Never man endured more painful mental and bodily agonies that he might secure for himself an assured spiritual peace. Romanists have expressed their wonder that so pure a man thought himself so great a sinner. But a sinner he was, as we all; and to avert the just anger of God he fasted, prayed, and mortified himself like an anchorite of the Thebaid. And yet no peace or comfort came.

A chained Bible lay in the monastery. He had previously found a copy of it in the library of the university. Day and night he read it, along with the writings of St. Augustine. In both he found the same pictures of man's depravity which he realized in himself, but God's remedy for sin he had not found. In the earnestness of his studies the prescribed devotions were betimes crowded out, and then he punished himself without mercy to redeem his failures. Whole nights and days together he lay upon his face crying to God, till he swooned in his agony. Everything his brother-monks could tell him he tried, but all the resources of their religion were powerless to comfort him or to beget a righteousness in which his anguished soul could trust.

It happened that one of the exceptionally enlightened and spiritual-minded monks of his time, ***John Staupitz***, was then the vicar-general of the Augustinians in Saxony. On his tour of inspection he came to Erfurt, and there found Luther, a walking skeleton, more dead than alive. He was specially drawn to the haggard young brother. The genial and sympathizing spirit of the vicar-general made Luther feel at home in his presence, and to him he freely opened his whole heart, telling of his feelings, failures, and fears--his heartaches, his endeavors, his disappointments, and his despair. And God put the right words into the vicar-general's mouth.

"Look to the wounds of Jesus," said he, "and to the blood he shed for you, and there see the mercy of God. Cast yourself into the Redeemer's arms, and trust in his righteous life and sacrificial death. He loved you first; love him in return, and let your penances and mortifications go."

The oppressed and captive spirit began to feel its burden lighten under such discourse. God a God of love! Piety a life of love! Salvation by loving trust in a God already reconciled in Christ! This was a new revelation. It brought the sorrowing young Luther to the study of the Scriptures with a new object of search. He read and meditated, and began to see the truth of what his vicar said. But doubts would come, and often his gloom returned.

One day an aged monk came to his cell to comfort him. He said he only knew his Creed, but in that he rested, reciting, "*I believe in the forgiveness of sins*."--"And do I not believe that?" said Luther.--"Ah," said the old monk, "you believe in the forgiveness of sins for David and Peter and the thief on the cross, but you do not believe in the forgiveness of sins *for yourself*. St. Bernard says the Holy Ghost speaks it to your own soul, *Thy* sins are forgiven *thee*."

And so at last the right nerve was touched. The true word of God's deliverance was brought home to Luther's understanding. He was penitent and in earnest, and needed only this great Gospel hope to lift him from the horrible pit and the miry clay. As a light from heaven it came to his soul, and there remained, a comfort and a joy. The glad conclusion flashed upon him, never more to be shaken, "If God, for Christ's sake, takes away our sins, then they are not taken away by any works of ours."

The foundation-rock of a new world was reached.

Luther saw not yet what all this discovery meant, nor whither it would lead. He was as innocent of all thought of being a Reformer as a new-born babe is of commanding an army on the battlefield. But the Gospel principle of deliverance and salvation for his oppressed and anxious soul was found, and it was found for all the world. The anchor had taken hold on a new continent. In essence the Great Reformation was born--born in Luther's soul.

LUTHER'S DEVELOPMENT.

More than ten years passed before this new principle began to work off the putrid carcass of mediaeval religion which lay stretched over the stifled and suffocating Church of Christ. There were yet many steps and stages in the preparation for what was to come. But from that time forward everything moved toward general regeneration by means of that marrow doctrine of the Gospel: ***Salvation by loving faith in the merit and mediation of Jesus alone***.

Staupitz counseled the young monk to study the Scriptures well and whatever could aid him in their right understanding, and gave orders to the monastery not to interfere with his studies.

On May 2, 1507, he was consecrated to the priesthood.

Within the year following, at the instance of Staupitz, Frederick the Wise appointed him professor in the new University of Wittenberg.

May 9, 1509, he took his degree of bachelor of divinity. From that time he began to use his place to attack the falsehoods of the prevailing philosophy and to explore and expose the absurdities of Scholasticism, dwelling much on the great Gospel treasure of God's free amnesty to sinful man through the merits and mediation of Jesus Christ, on which his own soul was planted.

Staupitz was astounded at the young brother's thorough mastery of the sacred Word, the minuteness of his knowledge of it, and the power with which he expounded and defended the great principles of the evangelic faith. So able a teacher of the doctrines of the cross must at once begin to preach. Luther remonstrated, for it was not then the custom for all priests to preach. He insisted that he would die under the weight of such responsibilities. "Die, then," said Staupitz; "God has plenty to do for intelligent young men in heaven."

A little old wooden chapel, daubed with clay, twenty by thirty feet in size, with a crude platform of rough boards at one end and a small sooty gallery for scarce twenty persons at the other, and propped on all sides to keep it from tumbling down, was assigned him as his cathedral. Myconius likens it to the stable of Bethlehem, as there Christ was born anew for the souls which now crowded to it. And when the thronging audiences required his transfer to the parish church, it was called the bringing of Christ into the temple.

The fame of this young theologian and preacher spread fast and far. The common people and the learned were alike impressed by his originality and power, and rejoiced in the electrifying clearness of his expositions and teachings. The Elector was delighted, for he began to see his devout wishes realized. Staupitz, who had drunk in the more pious spirit of the Mystic theologians, shared the same feeling, and saw in Luther's fresh, biblical, and energetic preaching what he felt the whole

Church needed. "He spared neither counsel nor applause," for he believed him the man of God for the times. He sent him to neighboring monasteries to preach to the monks. He gave him every opportunity to study, observe, and exercise his great talents. He even sent him on a mission to Rome, more to acquaint him with that city, which he longed to see, than for any difficult or pressing business with the pope.

LUTHER'S VISIT TO ROME.

Luther performed the journey on foot, passing from monastery to monastery, noting the extravagances, indolence, gluttony, and infidelity of the monks, and sometimes in danger of his life, both from the changes of climate and from the murderous resentments of some of these cloister-saints which his rebukes of their vices engendered.

When Rome first broke upon his sight, he hailed it reverently as the city of saints and holy martyrs. He almost envied those whose parents were dead, and who had it in their power to offer prayers for the repose of their souls by the side of such holy shrines. But when he beheld the vulgarities, profanities, paganism, and unconcealed unbelief which pervaded even the ecclesiastical circles of that city, his soul sunk within him.

There was much to be seen in Rome; and the Roman Catholic writers find great fault with Luther for being so dull and unappreciative as to move amid it without being touched with a single spark of poetic fire. They tell of the glory of the cardinals, in litters, on horseback, in glittering carriages, blazing with jewels and shaded with gorgeous canopies; of marble palaces, grand walks, alabaster columns, gigantic obelisks, villas, gardens, grottoes, flowers, fountains, cascades; of churches adorned with polished pillars, gilded soffits, mosaic floors, altars sparkling with diamonds, and gorgeous pictures from master-hands looking down from every wall; of monuments, statues, images, and holy relics; and they blame Luther that he could gaze upon it all without a stir of admiration--that he could look upon the sculpture and statuary and see nothing but pagan devices, the gods Demosthenes and Praxiteles, the feasts and pomps of Delos, and the idle scenes of the heathen Forum--that no gleam from the crown of Perugino or Michael Angelo dazzled his eyes, and no strain of Virgil or of Dante, which the people sung in the streets, attracted his ear-- that he was only cold and dumb before all the treasures and glories of art and all the grandeur of the high dignitaries of the Church, seeing nothing, feeling nothing, exclaiming over nothing but the licentious impurities of the priests, the pagan pomps of the pontiff, the profane jests of the ministers of religion, the bare shoulders of the Roman ladies.

Luther was not dead to the aesthetic, but to see faith and righteousness thus smothered and buried under a godless Epicurean life was an offence to his honest German conscience. It looked to him as if the popes had reversed the Saviour's choice, and accepted the devil's bid for Christ to worship him. From what his own eyes and ears had now seen and heard, he knew what to believe concerning the state of things in the metropolis of Christendom, and was satisfied that, as surely as there is a hell, the Rome of those days was its mouth.[3]

Note:

[3] Bellarmine, an honored author of the Roman Church, one competent to judge concerning the state of things at that time, and not over-forward to confess it, says: "For some years before the Lutheran and Calvinistic heresies were published there was not (as contemporary authors testify) any rigor in ecclesiastical judicatories, any discipline with regard to morals, any knowledge of sacred literature, any reverence for divine things: THERE WAS ALMOST NO RELIGION REMAINING."--***Bellarm.***, Concio xviii., Opera, tom. vi. col. 296, edit. Colon., 1617, apud ***Gerdesii Hist. Evan. Renovati***, vol. i. p. 25.

LUTHER AS TOWN-PREACHER.

On his return the Senate of Wittenberg elected him town-preacher. In the cloister, in the castle chapel, and in the collegiate church he alternately exercised his gifts. Romanists admit that "his success was great. He said he would not imitate his predecessors, and he kept his word. For the first time a Christian preacher was seen to abandon the Schoolmen and draw his texts and illustrations from the writings of inspiration. He was the originator and restorer of expository preaching in modern times."

The Elector heard him, and was filled with admiration. An old professor, whom the people called "the light of the world," listened to him, and was struck with his wonderful insight, his marvelous imagination, and his massive solidity. And Wittenberg sprang into great renown because of him, for never before had been heard in Saxony such a luminous expositor of God's holy Word.

LUTHER MADE A DOCTOR.

On all hands it was agreed and insisted that he should be made a doctor of divinity. The costs were heavy, for simony was the order of the day and the pope exacted high prices for all church promotions; but the Elector paid the charges.

On the 18th of October, 1512, the degree was conferred. It was no empty title to Luther. It gave him liberties and rights which his enemies could not gainsay, and it laid on him obligations and duties which he never forgot. The obedience to the canons and the hierarchy which it exacted he afterward found inimical to Christ and the Gospel, and, as in duty bound, he threw it off, with other swaddling-bands of Popery. But there was in it the pledge "to devote his whole life to the study, exposition and defence of the Holy Scriptures." This he accepted, and ever referred to as his sacred charter and commission. Nor was it without significance that the great bell of Wittenberg was rung when proclamation of this investiture was made. As the ringing of the bell on the old State-house when the Declaration of Independence was passed proclaimed the coming liberties of the American colonies, so this sounding of the great bell of Wittenberg when Luther was made doctor of divinity proclaimed and heralded to the nations of the earth the coming deliverance of the enslaved Church. God's chosen servant had received his commission, and the better day was soon to dawn.

*   *   *   *   *

Henceforth Luther's labors and studies went forward with a new impulse and inspiration. Hebrew and Greek were thoroughly mastered. The Fathers of the Church, ancient and modern, were carefully read. The systems of the Schoolmen, the Book of Sentences, the Commentaries, the Decretals--everything relating to his department as a doctor of theology--were examined, and brought to the test of Holy Scripture.

In his sermons, lectures, and disquisitions the results of these incessant studies came out with a depth of penetration, a clearness of statement, a simplicity of utterance, a devoutness of spirit, and a convincing power of eloquence which, with the eminent sanctity of his life, won for him unbounded praise. The common feeling was that the earth did not contain another such a doctor and had not seen his equal for many ages. Envy and jealousy themselves, those green-eyed monsters which gather about the paths of great qualities and successes, seemed for the time to be paralyzed before a brilliancy which rested on such humility, conscientiousness, fidelity, and merit.

LUTHER'S LABORS.

Years of fruitful labor passed. The Decalogue was expounded. Paul's letter to the Romans and the penitential Psalms were explained. The lectures on the Epistle to the Galatians were nearly completed. But no book from Luther had yet been published.

In 1515 he was chosen district vicar of the Augustinian monasteries of Meissen and Thuringia. It was a laborious office, but it gave him new experiences, familiarized him still more with the monks, brought him into executive administrations, and developed his tact in dealing with men.

One other particular served greatly to establish him in the hearts of the people. A deadly plague broke out in Wittenberg. Citizens were dying by dozens and scores. At a later period a like scourge visited Geneva, and so terrified Calvin and his ministerial associates that they appealed to the Supreme Council, entreating, "Mighty lords, release us from attending these infected people, for our lives are in peril." Not so Luther. His friends said, "Fly! fly!" lest he should fall by the plague and be lost to the world. "Fly?" said he. "No, no, my God. If I die, I die. The world will not perish because a monk has fallen. I am not St. Paul, not to fear death, but God will sustain me." And as an angel of mercy he remained, ministering to the sick and dying and caring for the orphans and widows of the dead.

COLLISION WITH THE HIERARCHY.

Such was Luther up to the time of his rupture with Rome. He knew something of the shams and falsities that prevailed, and he had assailed and exposed many of them in his lectures and sermons; but to lead a general reformation was the farthest from his thoughts. Indeed, he still had such confidence in the integrity of the Roman Church that he did not yet realize how greatly a thorough general reformation was needed. Humble in mind, peaceable in disposition, reverent toward authority, loving privacy, and fully occupied with his daily studies and duties, it was not in him to think of making war with powers whose claims he had not yet learned to question.

But it was not possible that so brave, honest, and self-sacrificing a man should long pursue his convictions without coming into collision with the Roman high priesthood. Though far off at Wittenberg, and trying to do his own duty well in his own legitimate sphere, it soon came athwart his path in a form so foul and offensive that it forced him to assault it. Either he had to let go his sincerest convictions and dearest hopes or protest had to come. His personal salvation and that of his flock were at stake, and he could in no way remain a true man and not remonstrate. Driven to this extremity, and struck at for his honest faithfulness, he struck again; and so came the battle which shook and revolutionized the world.

THE SELLING OF INDULGENCES.

Luther's first encounter with the hierarchy was on the traffic in indulgences. It was a good fortune that it there began. That traffic was so obnoxious to every sense of propriety that any vigorous attack upon it would command the approval of many honest and pious people. The central heresy of hierarchical religion was likewise embodied in it, so that a stab there, if logically followed up, would necessarily reach the very heart of the oppressive monster. And Providence arranged that there the conflict should begin.

Leo X. had but recently ascended the papal throne. Reared amid lavish wealth and culture, he was eager that his reign should equal that of Solomon and the Caesars. He sought to aggrandize his relatives, to honor and enrich men of genius, and to surround himself with costly splendors and pleasures. These demanded extraordinary revenues. The projects of his ambitious predecessors had depleted the papal coffers. He needed to do something on a grand scale in order adequately to replenish his exchequer.

As early as the eleventh century the popes had betimes resorted to the selling of pardons and the issuing of free passes to heaven on consideration of certain services or payments to the Church. From Urban II. to Leo X. this was more or less in vogue--first, to get soldiers for the holy wars,[4] and then as a means of wealth to the Church. If one wished to eat meat on fast-days, marry within prohibited degrees of relationship, or indulge in forbidden pleasures, he could do it without offence by rendering certain satisfactions before or after, which satisfactions could mostly be made by payments of money.[5] In the same way he could buy remission of sins in general, or exemption for so many days, years, or centuries from the pains of Purgatory. Bulls of authority were given, in the name of the Father, Son, and Holy Ghost, to issue certificates of exemption from all penalties to such as did the service or paid the equivalent. Immense incomes were thus realized. Even to the present this facile invention for raising money has not been entirely discontinued. Papal indulgences can be bought to-day in the shops of Spain and elsewhere.

Leo seized upon this system with all the vigor and unscrupulousness characteristic of the Medici. Had he been asked whether he really believed in these pardons, he would have said that the Church always believed the pope had power to grant them. Had he spoken his real mind in the matter, he would have said that if the people chose to be such fools, it was not for him to find fault with them. And thus, under plea of raising funds to finish St. Peter's, he instituted a grand trade in indulgences, and thereby laid the capstone of hierarchical iniquity which crushed the whole fabric to its base.

The right to sell these wares in Germany was awarded to Albert, the gay young prince-archbishop of Mayence. He was over head and ears in debt to the pope for his pallium, and Leo gave him this chance to get out.[6] Half the proceeds of the trade in his territory were to go to his credit. But the work of proclaiming and distributing the pardons was committed to **John Tetzel**, a Dominican prior who had long experience in the business, and who achieved "a forlorn notoriety in European history" by his zeal in prosecuting it.

Note:

[4] In the famous Bull of Gregory IX., published in 1234, that pope exhorts and commands all good Christians to take up the cross and join the expedition to recover the Holy Land. The language is: "The service to which mankind are now invited is an effectual atonement for the miscarriages of a negligent life. The discipline of a regular penance would have discouraged many offenders so much that they would have had no heart to venture upon it; but the holy war is a compendious method of discharging men from guilt and restoring them to the divine favor. Even if they die on their march, the intention will be taken for the deed, and many in this way may be crowned without fighting."--Given in Collier's *Eccl.*, vol. i.

[5] The Roman Chancery once put forth a book, which went through many editions, giving the exact prices for the pardon of each particular sin. A deacon guilty of murder was absolved for twenty pounds. A bishop or abbot might assas-

sinate for three hundred livres. Any ecclesiastic might violate his vows of chastity for the third part of that sum, etc., etc.--See Robertson's **Charles V.**

[6] The pallium, or pall, was a narrow band of white wool to go over the shoulders in the form of a circle, from which hung bands of similar size before and behind, finished at the ends with pieces of sheet lead and embroidered with crosses. It was the mark of the dignity and rank of archbishops. Albert owed Pope Leo X. forty-five thousand thalers for his right and appointment to wear the archbishop's pallium.

It was in this way that the Roman Church was accustomed to sell out benefices as a divine right. Even **expectative graces**, or mandates nominating a person to succeed to a benefice upon the first vacancy, were thus sold. Companies existed in Germany which made a business of buying up the benefices of particular sections and districts and retailing them at advanced rates. The selling of pardons was simply a lower kind of simoniacal bartering which pervaded the whole hierarchical establishment.

TETZEL'S PERFORMANCES.

Tetzel entered the towns with noise and pomp, amid waving of flags, singing, and the ringing of bells. Clergy, choristers, monks, and nuns moved in procession before and after him. He himself sat in a gilded chariot, with the Bull of his authority spread out on a velvet cushion before him.

The churches were his salesrooms, lighted and decorated for the occasion as in highest festival. From the pulpits his boisterous oratory rang, telling the virtues of indulgences, the wonderful power of the keys, and the unexampled grace of which he was the bearer from the holy lord and father at Rome.

He called on all--robbers, adulterers, murderers, everybody--to draw near, pay down their money, and receive from him letters, duly sealed, by which all their sins, past and future, should be pardoned and done away.

Not for the living only, but also for the dead, he proposed full and instantaneous deliverance from all future punishments on the payment of the price. And any wretch who dared to doubt or question the saving power of these certificates he in advance doomed to excommunication and the wrath of God.[7]

Catholic divines have labored hard to whitewash or explain away this stupendous iniquity; but, with all they have said or may say, such were the presentations made by the hawkers of these wares and such was the text of the diplomas they issued.

A dispensation or indulgence was nothing more nor less than a pretended letter of credit on Heaven, drawn at will by the pope out of the superabundant merits of Christ and all saints, to count so much on the books of God for so many murders, robberies, frauds, lies, slanders, or debaucheries. As the matter practically worked, a more profane and devilish traffic never had place in our world than that which the Roman hierarchy thus carried on in the name of the Triune God.

Note:

[7] Many of the sayings which Tetzel gave out in his addresses to the people have been preserved, and are amply attested by those who listened to his harangues.

"I would not," said he, "exchange my privileges for those of St. Peter in heaven. He saved many by his sermons; I have saved more by my indulgences."

"Indulgences are the most precious and sublime of all the gifts of God."

"No sins are so great that these pardons cannot cover them."

"Not for the living only, but for the dead also, there is immediate salvation in these indulgences."

"Ye priests, nobles, tradespeople, wives, maidens, young men! the souls of your parents and beloved ones are crying from the depths below: 'See our torments! A small alms would deliver us; and you can give it, and you will not.'"

"O dull and brutish people, not to appreciate the grace so richly offered! This day heaven is open on all sides, and how many are the souls you might redeem if you only would! Your father is in flames, and you can deliver him for ten groschen, and you do it not! What punishment must come for neglecting so great salvation! You should strip your coat from your back, if you have no other, and sell it to purchase so great grace as this, for God hath given all power to the pope."

"The bodies of St. Peter and St. Paul, with those of many blessed martyrs, lie exposed, trampled on, polluted, dishonored, and rotting in the weather. Our most holy lord the pope means to build the church to cover them with glory that shall have no equal on the earth. Shall those holy ashes be left to be trodden in the mire?"

"Therefore bring your money, and do a work most profitable to departed souls. Buy! buy!"

"This red cross with the pope's arms has equal virtue with the Cross of Christ."

"These pardons make cleaner than baptism, and purer than Adam was in his innocence in Paradise."

In the certificates which Tetzel gave to those who bought these pardons he declared that "by the authority of Jesus Christ, and of his apostles Peter and Paul, and of the most holy pope, I do absolve thee first from all ecclesiastical censures, in whatever manner they have been incurred, and then *from all thy sins, transgressions, and excesses, however enormous soever they may be*. I remit to you all punishment which you deserve in Purgatory on their account, and I restore you to the holy sacraments of the Church, union with the faithful, and to that innocence and purity possessed at baptism; *so that when you die the gates of punishment shall be shut and the gates of the happy Paradise shall be opened; and if your death shall be delayed, this grace shall remain in full force when you are at the point of death*."

The sums required for these passports to glory varied according to the rank and wealth of the applicant. For ordinary indulgence a king, queen, or bishop was to pay twenty-five ducats (a ducat being about a dollar of our money); abbots, counts, barons, and the like were charged ten ducats; other nobles and all who enjoyed annual incomes of five hundred florins were charged six ducats; and so down to half a florin, or twenty-five cents.

But the commissioner also had a special scale for taxes on particular sins. Sodomy was charged twelve ducats; sacrilege and perjury, nine; murder, seven or eight; witchcraft and polygamy, from two to six; taking the life of a parent, brother, sister, or an infant, from one to six.

LUTHER ON INDULGENCES.

Luther was on a tour of inspection as district vicar of the Augustinians when he first heard of these shameful doings. As yet he understood but little of the system, and could not believe it possible that the fathers at Rome could countenance, much less appoint and commission, such iniquities. Boiling with indignation for the honor of the Church, he threatened to make a hole in Tetzel's drum, and wrote to the authorities to refuse passports to the hucksters of these shameful deceptions.

But Tetzel soon came near to Wittenberg. Some of Luther's parishioners heard him, and bought absolutions. They afterward came to confession, acknowledging great irregularities of life. Luther rebuked their wickedness, and would not promise them forgiveness unless contrite for their sins and earnestly endeavoring to amend their evil ways. They remonstrated, and brought out their certificates of plenary pardon. "I have nothing to do with your papers," said he. "God's Word says you must repent and lead better lives, or you will perish."

His words were at once carried to the ears of Tetzel, who fumed with rage at such impudence toward the authority of the Church. He ascended the pulpit and hurled the curses of God upon the Saxon monk.

*   *   *   *   *

Thus an honest pastor finds some of his flock on the way to ruin, and tries to guide them right. He is not thinking of attacking Rome. He is ready to fight and die for holy Mother Church. His very protests are in her behalf. He is on his own rightful field, in faithful pursuit of his own rightful duty. Here the erring hierarchy seeks him out and attacks him. Shall he yield to timid fears and weak advisers, keep silence in his own house, and let the souls he is placed to guard become a prey to the destroyer? Is he not sworn to defend God's holy Word and Gospel? What will be his eternal fate and that of his people should he now hold his peace?

SERMON ON INDULGENCES.

Without conferring with flesh and blood his resolve was made--a resolve on which hung all the better future of the world--a resolve to take the pulpit against the lying indulgences.

For several days he shut himself in his cell to make sure of his ground and to elaborate what he would say. With eminent modesty and moderation his sentences were wrought, but with a perspicuity and clearness which no one could mistake. A crowded church awaited their delivery. He entered with his brother-monks, and joined in all the service with his usual voice and gravity. Nothing in his countenance or manner betrayed the slightest agitation of his soul. It was a solemn and momentous step for himself and for mankind that he was about to take, but he was as calmly made up to it as to any other duty of his life. The moment came for him to speak; ***and he spoke***.

"I hold it impossible," said he, "to prove from the Holy Scriptures that divine justice demands from the sinner any other penance or satisfaction than a true repentance, a change of heart, a willing submission to bear the Saviour's cross, and a readiness to do what good he can.

"That indulgences applied to souls in Purgatory serve to remit the punishments which they would otherwise suffer is an opinion devoid of any foundation.

"Indulgences, so far from expiating or cleansing from sin, leave the man in the same filth and condemnation in which they find him.

"The Church exacts somewhat of the sinner, and what it on its own account exacts it can on its own account remit, but nothing more.

"If you have aught to spare, in God's name give it for the building of St. Peter's, but do not buy pardons.

"If you have means, feed the hungry, which is of more avail than piling stones together, and far better than the buying of indulgences.

"My advice is, Let indulgences alone; leave them to dead and sleepy Christians; but see to it that ye be not of that kind.

"Indulgences are neither commanded nor approved of God. They excite no one to sanctification. They work nothing toward salvation.

"That indulgences have virtue to deliver souls from Purgatory I do not believe, nor can it be proven by them that teach it; the Church says nothing to that effect.

"What I preach to you is based on the certainty of the Holy Scriptures, which no one ought to doubt."

So Luther preached, and his word went out to the ends of the earth. It was no jest, like Ulric von Huetten's **Epistles of Obscure Men**, or like the ridicule which Reuchlin and Erasmus heaped upon the stupid monks. It raised no laugh, but penetrated, like a rifle-shot, into the very heart of things.

Those who listened were deeply affected by the serious boldness of the preacher. The audience was with him in conviction, but many trembled for the result. "Dear doctor, you have been very rash; what trouble may come of this!" said a venerable father as he pulled the sleeve of Luther's gown and shook his head with misgivings. "If this is not rightly done in God's name," said Luther, "it will come to nothing; if it is, let come what will."

It was honest duty to God, truth, and the salvation of men that moved him. Cowardly policy or timid expediency in such a matter was totally foreign to his soul.

In a few days, the substance of the sermon was in print. Tetzel raved over it. Melanchthon says he burnt it in the market-place of Jueterbock. In the name of God and the pope he bade defiance to its author, and challenged him by fire and water. Luther laughed at him for braying so loud at a distance, yet declining to come to Wittenberg to argue out the matter in close lists.

APPEAL TO THE BISHOPS.

Anxious to vindicate the Church from what he believed to be an unwarranted liberty in the use of her name, Luther wrote to the bishop of Brandenburg and the archbishop of Mayence. He made his points, and appealed to these his superiors to put down the scandalous falsities advanced by Tetzel. They failed to answer in any decisive way. The one timidly advised silence, and the other had too much pecuniary interest in the business to notice the letter.

Thus, as a pastor, Luther had taken his ground before his parishioners in the confessional. As a preacher he had uttered himself in earnest admonition from the pulpit. As a loyal son he had made his presentation and appeal to those in authority over him. Was he right? or was he wrong? No commanding answer came, and there remained one other way of testing the question. As a doctor of divinity he could lawfully, as custom had been, demand an open and fair discussion of the matter with teachers and theologians. And upon this he now resolved.

THE NINETY-FIVE THESES.

He framed a list of propositions on the points in question. They were in Latin, for his appeal was to theologians, and not yet to the common heart and mind of Germany. To make them public, he took advantage of a great festival at Wittenberg, when the town was full of visitors and strangers, and nailed them to the door of the new castle church, October 31, 1517.

These were the famous ***Ninety-five Theses***. They were plainly-worded statements of the same points he had made in the confessional and in his sermon. They contained no assault upon the Church, no arraignment of the pope, no personal attack on any one. Neither were they given as necessarily true, but as what Luther believed to be true, and the real truth or falsity of which he desired to have decided in the only way questions of faith and salvation can be rightly decided.

The whole matter was fairly, humbly, and legitimately put. "I, Martin Luther, Augustinian at Wittenberg," he added at the end, "hereby declare that I have written these propositions against indulgences. I understand that some, not knowing what they affirm, are of opinion that I am a heretic, though our renowned university has not condemned me, nor any temporal or spiritual authority. Therefore, now again, as often heretofore, I beg of one and all, for the sake of the true Christian faith, to show me the better way, if peradventure they have learned it from above, or at least to submit their opinion to the decision of God and the Church; for I am not so insane as to set up my views above everything and everybody, nor so silly as to accept the fables invented by men in preference to the Word of God."

It is from the nailing up of these *Theses* that the history of the Great Reformation dates; for the hammer-strokes which fixed that parchment started the Alpine avalanche which overwhelmed the pride of Rome and broke the stubborn power which had reigned supreme for a thousand years.

EFFECT OF THE THESES.

As no one came forward to discuss his Theses, Luther resolved to publish them to the world.

In fourteen days they overspread Germany. In a month they ran through all Christendom. One historian says it seemed as if the angels of God were engaged in spreading them.

At a single stroke, made in modesty and faith, Luther had become the most noted person in Germany--the man most talked of in all the world--the mouthpiece of the best people in Christendom--the leader of a mighty revolution.

Reuchlin read, and thanked God.

Erasmus read, and rejoiced, only counseling moderation and prudence.

The Emperor Maximilian read, and wrote to the Saxon Elector: "Take care of the monk Luther, for the time may come when we will need him."

The bishop of Wurzburg read, and was filled with gladness, and wrote to the Elector Frederick to hold on to Luther as a preacher of the truth of God.

The prior of Steinlausitz read, and could not suppress his joy. "See here," said he to his monks: "the long-waited-for has come; he tells the truth. *Berg* means mountain, and *Wittenberg* is the mountain whither all the world will come to seek wisdom, and will find it."

A student of Annaberg read, and said, "This Luther is the reaper in my dream, whom the voice bade me follow and gather in the bread of life;" and from that hour he was a fast friend of Luther and his cause, and became the distinguished Myconius.

The pope himself read the Theses, and did not think unfavorably of their author. He saw in Luther a man of learning and brilliant genius, and that pleased him. The questions mooted he referred to a mere monkish jealousy--an unsober gust of passion which would soon blow over. He did not then realize the seriousness which was in the matter. His sphere was heathen art and worldly magnificence, not searching into the ways of God's salvation.

The great German heart was moved, and the brave daring of him whose voice was thus lifted up against the abominations which were draining the country to fill the pope's coffers was hailed with enthusiasm. Had Luther been a smaller man he would have been swept away by his vast and sudden fame.

But not all was sunshine. Erasmus wittily said, Luther committed two unpardonable sins: he touched the pope's crown and the monks' bellies. Such effrontery would needs raise a mighty outcry.

Prierias, the master of the sacred palace, pronounced Luther a heretic. Hochstrat of Cologne, Reuchlin's enemy, clamored for fire to burn him. The indulgence-venders thundered their anathemas, promising a speedy holocaust of Luther's body. The monasteries took on the form of so many kennels of enraged hounds howling to each other across the spiritual waste. And even some who pronounced the Theses scriptural and orthodox shook their heads and sought to quash such dangerous proceedings.

But Luther remained firm at his post. He honestly believed what he had written, and he was not afraid of the truth. If the powers of the world should come down upon him and kill him, he was prepared for the slaughter. In all the mighty controversy he was ever ready to serve the Gospel with his life or with his death.

TETZEL'S END.

Tetzel continued to bray and fume against him from pulpit and press, denouncing him as a heresiarch, heretic, and schismatic. By Wimpina's aid he issued a reply to Luther's sermon, and also counter-theses on Luther's propositions. But the tide was turning in the sea of human thinking. Luther's utterances had turned it. The people were ready to tear the mountebank to pieces. Two years later he imploringly complained to the pope's nuncio, Miltitz, that such fury pursued him in Germany,

Bohemia, Hungary, and Poland that he was nowhere safe. Even the representative of the pope gave the wretch no sympathy. When Luther heard of his illness he sent him a letter to tell him that he had forgiven him all. He died in Leipsic, neglected, smitten in soul, and full of misery, July 14, 1519.

LUTHER'S GROWING INFLUENCE.

Six months after the nailing up of the Theses, Luther was the hero of a general convention of the Augustinians in Heidelberg. He there submitted a series of propositions on philosophy and theology, which he defended with such convincing clearness and tact that he won for himself and his university great honor and renown. Better still, four learned young men who there heard him saw the truth of his positions, and afterward became distinguished defenders of the Reformation.

His cause, meanwhile, was rapidly gaining friends. His replies to Tetzel, Prierias, Hochstrat, and Eck had gone forth to deepen the favorable impression made by the Ninety-five Theses. Truth had once more lifted up its head in Europe, and Rome would find it no child's play to put it down. The skirmish-lines of the hierarchy had been met and driven in. The tug of serious battle was now to come.

HIS APPEAL TO THE POPE.

Luther made the advance. He wrote out explanations (or "*Resolutions*") of his Theses, and sent them, with a letter, to the pope. With great confidence, point, and elegance, but with equal submissiveness and humility, he spoke of the completeness of Christ for the salvation of every true believer, without room or need for penances and other satisfactions; of the evilness of the times, and the pressing necessity for a general reform; of the damaging complaints everywhere resounding against the traffic in indulgences; of his unsuccessful appeals to the ecclesiastical princes; and of the unjust censures being heaped upon him for what he had done, entreating His Holiness to instruct his humble petitioner, and condemn or approve, kill or preserve, as the voice of Christ through him might be. He then believed that God's sanction had to come through the high clergy and heads of the Church. Many good Christians had approved his Theses, but he did not recognize in that the divine answer to his testimony. He said afterward: "I looked only to the pope, the cardinals, the bishops, the theologians, the jurisconsults, the monks, the priests, from whom I expected the breathing of the Spirit." He had not yet learned what a bloody dragon claimed to impersonate the Lamb of God.

CITATION TO ANSWER FOR HERESY.

While, in open frankness, Luther was thus meekly committing himself to the powers at Rome, **they** were meditating his destruction. Insidiously they sought to deprive him of the Elector's protection, and answered his humble and confiding appeal with a citation to appear before them to answer for heresy.

Things now were ominous of evil. Wittenberg was filled with consternation. If Luther obeyed, it was evident he would perish like so many faithful men before him; if he refused, he would be charged with contumacy and involve his prince. One and another expedient were proposed to meet the perplexity; but to secure a hearing in Germany was all Luther asked.

To this the pope proved more willing than was thought. He was not sure of gaining by the public trial and execution of a man so deeply planted in the esteem of his countrymen, and by bringing him before a prudent legate he might induce him to retract and the trouble be ended; if not, it would be a less disturbing way of getting possession of the accused man. Orders were therefore issued for Luther to appear before Cardinal Cajetan at Augsburg.

LUTHER BEFORE CAJETAN.

On foot he undertook the journey, believed by all to be a journey to his death. But Maximilian, then in the neighborhood of Augsburg, gave him a safe-conduct, and Cajetan was obliged to receive him with civility. He even embraced him with tokens of affection, thinking to win him to retraction. Luther was much softened by these kindly manifestations, and was disposed to comply with almost anything if not required to deny the truth of God.

The interviews were numerous. Luther was told that it was useless to think that the civil powers would go to war for his protection; and where would he then be? His answer was: "I will be, as now, under the broad heavens of the Almighty." Remonstrances, entreaties, threatenings, and proposals of high distinction were addressed to him; but he wanted no cardinal's hat, and for nothing in Rome's power would he consent to retract what he believed to be the Gospel truth till shown wherein it was at variance with the divine Word. Cajetan's arguments tripped and failed at every point, and he could only reiterate that he had been sent to receive a retraction, not to debate the questions. Luther as often promised this when shown from the Scriptures to be in the wrong, but not till then.

CAJETAN'S MORTIFICATION.

Foiled and disappointed in his designs, and astounded and impatient that a poor monk should thus set at naught all the prayers and powers of the sovereign of Christendom, the cardinal bade him see his face no more until he had repented of his stubbornness.

At this the friends of the Reformer, fearing for his safety, clandestinely hurried him out of Augsburg, literally grappling him up from his bed only half dressed, and brought him away to his university. He had answered the pope's summons, and yet was free!

Cajetan was mortified at the result, and was upbraided for his failure. In his chagrin he wrote angrily to the Elector not to soil his name and lineage by sheltering a heretic, but to surrender Luther at once, on pain of an interdict. The Elector was troubled. Luther had not been proven a heretic, neither did he believe him to be one; but he feared collision with the pope.

Luther said if he were in the Elector's place he would answer the cardinal as he deserved for thus insulting an honest man; but, not to be an embarrassment to his prince, he agreed to leave the Elector's dominions if he said so. But Frederick would not surrender his distinguished subject to the legate, neither would he send him out of the country. It is hard to say which was here the nobler man, Luther or his illustrious protector.

PROGRESS OF EVENTS.

The minds of men by this time were much aroused, and Luther's cause grew and strengthened. The learned Melanchthon, Reuchlin's relative and pupil, was added to the faculty at Wittenberg, and became Luther's chief co-laborer. The number of students in the university swelled to thousands, including the sons of noblemen and princes from all parts, who listened with admiration to Luther's lectures and sermons and spread his fame and doctrines. And the feeling was deep and general that a new and marvelous light had arisen upon the world.[8]

It was now that Maximilian died (Jan. 17, 1519), and Charles V., his grandson, a Spanish prince of nineteen years, succeeded to his place. The Imperial crown was laid at the feet of the Elector Frederick, Luther's friend, but he declined it in favor of Charles, only exacting a solemn pledge that he would not disturb the liberties of Germany. Civil freedom is one of the glorious fruits of the Reformation, and here already it began to raise barricades against despotic power.

Note:

[8] A writer of the Roman Church, in a vein of somewhat mingled sarcasm and seriousness, remarks: "The university had reason to be proud of Luther, whose oral lectures attracted a multitude of strangers; these pilgrims from distant quarters joined their hands and bowed their heads at the sight of the towers of the city, like other travelers before Jerusalem. Wittenberg was like a new Zion, whence the light of truth expanded to neighboring kingdoms, as of old from the Holy City to pagan nations."

THE LEIPSIC DISPUTATION.

Up to this time, however, there had been no questioning of the divine rights claimed by the hierarchy. Luther was still a Papist, and thought to grow his plants of evangelic faith under the shadow of the Upas of ecclesiasticism. He had not yet been brought to see how his Augustinian theology concerning sin and grace ran afoul of the entire round of the mediaeval system and methods of holiness. It was only the famous Leipsic Disputation between him and Dr. John Eck that showed him the remoter and deeper relations of his position touching indulgences.

This otherwise fruitless debate had the effect of making the nature and bearings of the controversy clear to both sides. Eck now distinctly saw that Luther must be forcibly put down or the whole papal system must fall; and Luther was made to realize that he must surrender his doctrine of salvation through simple faith in Christ or break with the pope and the hierarchical system.

Accepting the pontifical doctrines as true, Eck claimed the victory, because he had driven Luther to expressions at variance with those doctrines. On the other hand, Luther had shown that the pontifical claims were without foundation in primitive Christianity or the Holy Scriptures; that the Papacy was not of divine authority or of the essence of the Church; that the Church existed before and beyond the papal hierarchy, as well as under it; that the only Head of the universal Christian Church is Christ himself; that wherever there is true faith in God's Word, there the Church is, whatever the form of external organization; that the popes could err and had erred, and councils likewise; and that neither separately nor together could they rightfully decree or ordain contrary to the Scriptures, the only infallible Rule.

To all this Eck could make no answer except that it was Hussism over again, which the Council of Constance had condemned, and that, from the standpoint of the hierarchy, Luther was a heretic and ought to be dealt with accordingly.

RESULTS FROM THE DEBATE.

Luther now realized that the true Gospel of God's salvation and the pontifical system were vitally and irreconcilably antagonistic; that the one could never be held in consistency with the other; and that there must come a final break between him and Rome. This much depressed him. He showed his spiritual anguish by his deep dejection. But he soon rose above it. If he had the truth of God, as he verily believed, what were the pope and all devils against Jehovah? And so he went on lecturing, preaching, writing, and publishing with his greatest power, brilliancy, and effectiveness.

Some of the best and most telling products of his pen now went forth to multitudes of eager readers. The glowing energy of his faith acted like a spreading fire, kindling the souls of men as they seldom have been kindled in any cause in any age. His *Address to the Nobility* electrified all Germany, and first fired the patriotic spirit of Ulrich Zwingli, the Swiss Reformer. His book on *The Babylonian Captivity of the Church* sounded a bugle-note which thrilled through all the German heart, gave Bugenhagen to the Reformation, and sent a shudder through the hierarchy.[9] Already, at Maximilian's Diet at Augsburg to take measures against the Turk, a Latin pamphlet was openly circulated among the members which said that the Turk to be resisted was living in Italy; and Miltitz, the pope's nuncio and chamberlain, confessed that from Rome to Altenberg he had found those greatly in the minority who did not side with Luther.

Note:

[9] Glapio, the confessor of Charles V., stated to Chancellor Brueck at the Diet of Worms: "The alarm which I felt when I read the first pages of the *Captivity* cannot be expressed; they might be said to be lashes which scourged me from head to foot."

LUTHER'S EXCOMMUNICATION.

But the tempest waxed fiercer and louder every day. Luther's growing influence the more inflamed his enemies. Hochstrat had induced two universities to condemn his doctrines. In sundry places his books were burned by the public hangman. Eck had gone to Italy, and was "moving the depths of hell" to secure the excommunication of the prejudged heretic. And could his bloodthirsty enemies have had their way, this would long since have come. But Leo seems to have had more respect for Luther than for them. Learning and talent were more to him than any doctrines of the faith. The monks complained of him as too much given to luxury and pleasure to do his duty in defending the Church. Perhaps he had conscience enough to be ashamed to enforce his traffic in paper pardons by destroying the most honest and heroic man in Germany. Perhaps he did not like to stain his reign with so foul a record, even if dangerous complications should not attend it. Whatever the cause, he was slow to respond to these clamors for blood. Eck had almost as much trouble to get him to issue the Bull of Luther's excommunication as he had to answer Luther's arguments in the Leipsic Discussion. But he eventually procured it, and undertook to enforce it.

And yet, with all his zealous personal endeavors and high authority, he could hardly get it posted, promulged, or at all respected in Germany. His parchment thunder lost its power in coming across the Alps. Miltitz also was in his way, who, with equal authority from the pope, was endeavoring to supersede the Bull by attempts at reconciliation. It came to Wittenberg in such a sorry plight that Luther laughed at it as having the appearance of a forgery by Dr. Eck. He knew the pope had been bullied into the issuing of it, but this was the biting irony by which he indicated the character of the men by whom it was moved and the pitiable weakness to which such thunders had been reduced.

But it was a Bull of excommunication nevertheless. Luther and his doctrines were condemned by the chief of Christendom.[10] Multitudes were thrown into anxious perturbation. If the strong arm of the emperor should be given to sustain the pope, who would be able to stand? Adrian, one of the faculty of Wittenberg, was so frightened that he threw down his office and hastened to join the enemy.

Amid the perils which surrounded Luther powerful knights offered to defend him by force of arms; but he answered, "*No*; by *the Word* the world was conquered, by *the Word* the Church was saved, and by *the Word* it must be restored." The thoughts of his soul were not on human power, but centred on the throne of Him who lives for ever. It was Christ's Gospel that was in peril, and he was sure Jehovah would not abandon his own cause.

Germany waited to see what he would do. Nor was it long kept in suspense.

Note:

[10] The Bull was issued June 15, 1520. It specified forty-one propositions out of Luther's works which it condemned as heretical, scandalous, and offensive to pious ears. It forbade all persons to read his writings, upon pain of excommunication. Such as had any of his books in their possession were commanded to burn them. He himself, if he did not publicly recant his errors and burn his books within sixty days, was pronounced an obstinate heretic, excommunicated and delivered over to Satan. And it enjoined upon all secular princes, under pain of incurring the same censure, to seize his person and deliver him up to be punished as his crimes deserved; that is to be burnt as a heretic.

LUTHER AND THE POPE'S BULL.

In a month he discharged a terrific volley of artillery upon the Papacy by his book *Against the Bull of Antichrist*.

In thirteen days later he brought formal charges against the pope--*first*, as an unjust judge, who condemns without giving a hearing; *second*, as a heretic and apostate, who requires denial that faith is necessary; *third*, as an Antichrist, who sets himself against the Holy Scriptures and usurps their authority; and *fourth*, as a blasphemer of the Church and its free councils, who declares them nothing without himself.

This was carrying the war into Africa. Appealing to a future general council and the Scriptures as superior to popes, he now called upon the emperor, electors, princes, and all classes and estates in the whole German empire, as they valued the Gospel and the favor of Christ, to stand by him in this demonstration.

And, that all might be certified in due form, he called a notary and five witnesses to hear and attest the same as verily the solemn act and deed of Martin Luther, done in behalf of himself and all who stood or should stand with him.

Rome persisted in forcing a schism, and this was Luther's bill of divorcement.

Nay, more; as Rome had sealed its condemnation of him by burning his books, he built a stack of fagots on the refuse piles outside the Elster Gate of Wittenberg, invited thither the whole university, and when the fires were kindled and the flames were high, he cast into them, one by one, the books of the canon law, the Decretals, the Clementines, the Papal Extravagants, and all that lay at the base of the religion of the hierarchy! And when these were consumed he took Leo's Bull of excommunication, held it aloft, exclaiming with a loud voice, "Since thou hast afflicted the saints of God, be thou consumed with fire unquenchable!" and dashed the impious document into the flames.

Well done was that! Luther considered it the best act of his life. It was a brave heart, the bravest then living in this world, that dared to do it. But it was done then and for ever. Wittenberg looked on with shoutings. The whole modern world of civilized man has ever since been looking on with thrilling wonder. And myriads of the sons of God and liberty are shouting over it yet.

The miner's son had come up full abreast with the triple-crowned descendant of the Medici. The monk of Wittenberg had matched the proudest monarch in the world. Henceforth the question was, Which of them should sway the nations in the time to come?

THE DIET OF WORMS.

The young emperor sided with the religion of the pope. The venerable Elector Frederick determined to stand by Luther, at least till his case was fairly adjudged. He said it was not just to condemn a good and honest man unheard and unconvicted, and that "*Justice must take precedence even of the pope*."

Conferences of state now became numerous and exciting, and the efforts of Rome to have Luther's excommunication recognized and enforced were many and various, but nothing short of a Diet of the empire could settle the disturbance.[11]

Such a Diet was convoked by the young emperor for January, 1521. It was the first of his reign, and the grandest ever held on German soil. Philip of Hesse came to it with a train of six hundred cavaliers. The electors, dukes, archbishops, landgraves, margraves, counts, bishops, barons, lords, deputies, legates, and ambassadors from foreign courts came in corresponding style. They felt it important to show their consequence at this first Diet, and were all the more moved to be there in force because the exciting matter of Reform was specified as one of the chief things to be considered. The result was one of the most august and illustrious assemblies of which modern history tells, and one which presented a spectacle of lasting wonder that a poor lone monk should thus have moved all the powers of the earth.

Note:

[11] Audin, in his *Life of Luther*, says: "A monk who wore a cassock out at the elbows had caused to the most powerful emperor in the world greater embarrass-

ments than those which Francis I., his unsuccessful rival at Frankfort, threatened to raise against him in Italy. With the cannon from his arsenal at Ghent and his lances from Namur, Charles could beat the king of France between sunrise and sunset; but lances and cannon were impotent to subdue the religious revolution, which, like some of the glaciers which he crossed in coming from Spain, acquired daily a new quantity of soil."--Vol. i. chap. 25. Again, in chap. 30, he says of the emperor: "The thought of measuring his strength with the hero of Marignan was far from alarming him, but a struggle with the monk of Wittenberg disturbed his sleep. He wished that they should try to overcome his obstinacy."

DOINGS OF THE ROMANISTS.

For three months the Diet wrangled over the affair of Luther without reaching anything decided. The friends of Rome were the chief actors, struggling in every way and hesitating at nothing to induce the Diet and the emperor to acknowledge and enforce the pope's decree. But the influence of the German princes, especially that of the Elector Frederick, stood in the way; Charles would not act, as he had no right to act, without the concurrence of the states, and the princes of Germany held it unjust that Luther should be condemned on charges which had never been fairly tried, on books which were not proven to be his, and especially since the sentence itself presented conditions with reference to which no answer had been legally ascertained.

To overcome these oppositions different resorts were tried. Leo issued a second Bull, excommunicating Luther absolutely, anathematizing him and all his friends and abettors. The pope's legate called for money to buy up influence for the Romanists: "We must have money. Send us money. Money! money! or Germany is lost!" The money came; but the Reformer's friends could not be bought with bribes, however much the agents of Rome needed such stimulation.

Trickery was brought into requisition to entrap Luther's defenders by a secret proposal to compromise. Luther was given great credit and right, except that he had gone a little too far, and it was only necessary to restrain him from further demonstrations. Rome compromise with a man she had doubly excommunicated and anathematized! Rome make terms with an outlaw whom she had infallibly doomed to eternal execration! Yet with these proposals the emperor's confessor approached Chancellor Brueck. But the chancellor's head was too clear to be caught by such treachery.

Then it was moved to refer the matter to a commission of arbitrators. This met with so much favor that the pope's legate, Aleander, was alarmed lest Luther should thereby escape, and hence set himself with unwonted energy to incite the emperor to decisive measures.

Charles was persuaded to make a demonstration, but demanded that the legate should first "convince the Diet." Aleander was the most famous orator Rome had, and he rejoiced in his opportunity. He went before the assembly in a prepared speech of three hours in length to show up Luther as a pestilent heretic, and the necessity of getting rid of him and his books and principles at once to prevent the world from being plunged into barbarism and utter desolation. He made a deep impression by his effort. It was only by the unexpected and crushing speech of Duke George of Saxony, Luther's bitter personal enemy, that the train of things, so energetically wrought up, was turned.

Not in defence of Luther, whom he disliked, but in defence of the German nation, he piled up before the door of the hierarchy such an overwhelming array of its oppressions, robberies, and scandals, and exposed with such an unsparing hand the falsities, profligacies, cupidity, and beastly indecencies of the Roman clergy and officials, that the emperor hastened to recall the edict he had already signed, and yielded consent for Luther to be called to answer for himself.

LUTHER SUMMONED.

In vain the pope's legate protested that it was not lawful thus to bring the decrees of the sovereign pontiff into question, or pleaded that Luther's daring genius, flashing eyes, electric speech, and thrilling spirit would engender tumult and violence. On March 6th the emperor signed a summons and safe-conduct for the Reformer to appear in Worms within twenty-one days, to answer concerning his doctrines and writings.

So far the thunders of the Vatican were blank.

With all the anxious fears which such a summons would naturally engender, Luther resolved to obey it.

The pope's adherents fumed in their helplessness when they learned that he was coming--coming, too, under the safe-conduct of the empire, coming to have a hearing before the Diet!--*he* whom the infallible Vicar of Heaven had condemned and anathematized! Whither was the world drifting?

Luther's friends trembled lest he should share the fate of Huss; his enemies trembled lest he should escape it; and both, in their several ways, tried to keep him back.

Placards of his condemnation were placed before him on the way, and spectacles to indicate his certain execution were enacted in his sight; but he was not the man to be deterred by the prospect of being burnt alive if God called for the sacrifice.

Lying fraud was also tried to seduce and betray him. Glapio, the emperor's confessor, who had tried a similar trick upon the Elector Frederick, conceived the idea that if Von Sickingen and Bucer could be won for the plot, a proposal to compromise the whole matter amicably might serve to beguile him to the chateau of his friend at Ebernburg till his safe-conduct should expire, and then the liars could throw off the mask and dispose of him with credit in the eyes of Rome. The glib and wily Glapio led in the attempt. Von Sickingen and Bucer were entrapped by his bland hypocrisy, and lent themselves to the execution of the specious proposition. But when they came to Luther with it, he turned his back, saying, "If the emperor's confessor has anything to say to me he will find me at Worms."

But even his friends were alarmed at his coming. It was feared that he would be destroyed. The Elector's confidential adviser sent a servant out to meet him, beseeching him by no means to enter the city. "Go tell your master," said Luther, "I will enter Worms though as many devils should be there as tiles upon its houses!" And he did enter, with nobles, cavaliers, and gentry for his escort, and attended through the streets by a larger concourse than had greeted the entry of the emperor himself.[12]

Note:

[12] "The reception which he met with at Worms was such as he might have reckoned a full reward of all his labors if vanity and the love of applause had been the principles by which he was influenced. Greater crowds assembled to behold him than had appeared at the emperor's public entry; his apartments were daily filled with princes and personages of the highest rank; and he was treated with all the respect paid to those who possess the power of directing the understanding and sentiments of other men--a homage more sincere, as well as more flattering, than

any which pre-eminence in birth or condition command."--Robertson's ***Charles V.***, vol. i. p. 510.

LUTHER AT THE DIET.

Charles hurried to convene his council, saying, "Luther is come; what shall we do with him?"

A chancellor and bishop of Flanders urged that he be despatched at once, and this scandalous humiliation of the Holy See terminated. He said Sigismund had allowed Huss to be burned, and no one was bound to keep faith with a heretic. But the emperor was more moral than the teachings of his Church, and said, "Not so; we have given our promise, and we ought to keep it."

On the morrow Luther was conducted to the Diet by the marshal of the empire. The excited people so crowded the gates and jammed about the doors that the soldiers had to use their halberds to open a way for him. An instinct not yet interpreted drew their hearts and allied them with the hero. From the thronged streets, windows, and housetops came voices as he passed--voices of petition and encouragement--voices of benediction on the brave and true--voices of sympathy and adjuration to be firm in God and in the power of his might. It was Germany, Scandinavia, England, Scotland, and Holland; it was the Americas and hundreds of young republics yet unborn; it was the whole world of all after-time, with its free Gospel, free conscience, free speech, free government, free science, and free schools,--uttering themselves in those half-smothered voices. Luther heard them and was strengthened.

But there was no danger he would betray the momentous trust. That morning, amid great rugged prayers which broke from him like massive rock-fragments hot and burning from a volcano of mingled faith and agony, laying one hand on the open Bible and lifting the other to heaven, he cast his soul on Omnipotence, in pledge unspeakable to obey only his conscience and his God. Whether for life or death, his heart was fixed.

A few steps more and he stood before Imperial majesty, encompassed by the powers and dignitaries of the earth, so brave, calm, and true a man that thrones and kings looked on in silent awe and admiration, and even malignant scorn for the moment retreated into darkness. Since He who wore the crown of thorns stood before Pontius Pilate there had not been a parallel to this scene.[13]

Note:

[13] A Romanist thus describes the picture: "When the approach of Luther was heard there ensued one of those deep silences in which the heart alone, by its hurried pulsations, gives sign of life. Attention was diverted from the emperor to the monk. On the appearance of Luther every one rose, regardless of the sovereign's presence. It inspired Werner with one of the finest acts of his tragedy.... Heine has glorified the appearance at Worms. The Catholic himself loves to contemplate that black gown in the presence of those lords and barons caparisoned in iron and armed with helmet and spear, and is moved by the voice of 'that young friar' who comes to defy all the powers of the earth."--Audin's *Life of Luther*.

"All parties must unite in admiring and venerating the man who, undaunted and alone, could stand before such an assembly, and vindicate with unshaken courage what he conceived to be the cause of religion, of liberty, and of truth, fearless of any reproaches but those of his own conscience, or of any disapprobation but that of his God."--Roscoe's *Life of Leo X.*, vol. iv. p. 36.

Luther himself, afterward recalling the event, said: "It must indeed have been God who gave me my boldness of heart; I doubt if I could show such courage again."

LUTHER'S REFUSAL TO RECANT.

A weak, poor man, arraigned and alone before the assembled powers of the earth, with only the grace of God and his cause on which to lean, had demand made of him whether or not he would retract his books or any part of them, *Yes* or *No*. But he did not shrink, neither did he falter. "Since Your Imperial Majesty and Your Excellencies require of me a direct and simple answer, I will give it. To the pope or councils I cannot submit my faith, for it is clear that they have erred and contradicted one another. Therefore, unless I am convinced by proofs from Holy Scripture or by sound reasons, and my judgment by this means is commanded by God's Word, *I cannot and will not retract anything*: for a Christian cannot safely go contrary to his conscience." And, glancing over the august assembly, on whose will his life hung, he added in deep solemnity, those immortal words: "HERE I STAND. I CAN DO NO OTHERWISE. SO HELP ME GOD! AMEN."[14]

Simple were the facts. Luther afterward wrote to a friend: "I expected His Majesty would bring fifty doctors to convict the monk outright; but it was not so. The whole history is this: Are these your books? *Yes.*--Will you retract them? *No.*--Well then, begone."

He said the truth, but he could not then know all that was involved in what he reduced to such a simple colloquy. With that *Yes* and *No* the wheel of ages made another revolution. The breath which spoke them turned the balances in which the whole subsequent history of civilization hung. It was the *Yes* and *No* which applied the brakes to the Juggernaut of usurpation, whose ponderous wheels had been crushing through the centuries. It was the *Yes* and *No* which evidenced the reality of a power above all popes and empires. It was the *Yes* and *No* which spoke the supreme obligation of the human soul to obey God and conscience, and started once more the pulsations of liberty in the arteries of man. It was the *Yes* and *No* which divided eras, and marked the summit whence the streams began to form and flow to give back to this world a Church without a pope and a State without an Inquisition.

Charles had the happiness at Worms to hear the tidings that Fernando Cortes had added Mexico to his dominions. The emancipated peoples of the earth in the generations since have had the happiness to know that at Worms, through the inflexible steadfastness of Martin Luther, God gave the inspirations of a new and better life for them!

Note:

[14] "With this noble protest was laid the keystone of the Reformation. The pontifical hierarchy shook to its centre, and the great cause of truth and regenerate religion spread with electric speed. The marble tomb of ignorance and error gave way, as it were, of a sudden; a thousand glorious events and magnificent discoveries thronged upon each other with pressing haste to behold and congratulate the mighty birth, the new creation, of which they were the harbingers, when, with a steady and triumphant step, the peerless form of human intellect rose erect, and, throwing off from its freshening limbs the death-shade and the grave-clothes by which it was enshrouded, ascended to the glorious resurrection of that noontide lustre which irradiates the horizon of our own day, rejoicing like a giant to run his race."--John Mason Good's *Book of Nature*, p. 321.

LUTHER'S CONDEMNATION.

After Luther and his friends left Worms the emperor issued an edict putting him and all his adherents under the ban of the empire, forbidding any one to give him food or shelter, calling on all who found him to arrest him, commanding all his books to be burned, and ordering the seizure of his friends and the confiscation of their possessions.

It was what Germany got for putting an Austro-Spanish bigot on the Imperial throne.

LUTHER IN THE WARTBURG.

But the cause of Rome was not helped by it. Luther's person was made safe by the Elector, who arranged a friendly capture by which he was concealed in the Wartburg in charge of the knights.

No one knew what had become of him. His mysterious disappearance was naturally referred to some foul play of the Romanists, and the feeling of resentment was intense and deep. Indeed, Germany was now bent on throwing off the religion of the hierarchy. No matter what it may once have been, no matter what service it may have rendered in helping Europe through the Dark Ages, it had become gangrened, perverted, rotten, offensive, unbearable. The very means Rome took to defend it increased revolt against it. It had come to be an oppressive lie, and it had to go. No Bulls of popes or edicts of emperors could alter the decree of destiny.

And a great and blessed fortune it was that Luther still lived to guide and counsel in the momentous transition. But Providence had endowed him for the purpose, and so preserved him for its execution. What was born with the Theses, and baptized before the Imperial Diet at Worms, he was now to nourish, educate, catechise, and prepare for glorious confirmation before a similar Diet in the after years.

TRANSLATION OF THE BIBLE.

While in the Wartburg he was forbidden to issue any writings. Leisure was thus afforded for one of the most important things connected with the Reformation. Those ten months he utilized to prepare for Germany and for the world a translation of the Holy Scriptures, which itself was enough to immortalize the Reformer's name. Great intellectual monuments have come down to us from the sixteenth century. It was an age in which the human mind put forth some of its noblest demonstrations. Great communions still look back to its Confessions as their rallying-centres, and millions of worshipers still render their devotions in the forms which then were cast. But pre-eminent over all the achievements of that sublime century was the giving of God's Word to the people in their own language, which had its chief centre and impulse in the production of Luther's **German Bible**. Well has it been said, "He who takes up that, grasps a whole world in his hand--a world which will perish only when this green earth itself shall pass away."

It was the Word that kindled the heart of Luther to the work of Reformation, and the Word alone could bring it to its consummation. With the Word the whole Church of Christ and the entire fabric of our civilization must stand or fall. Undermine the Bible and you undermine the world. It is the one, true, and only Charter of Faith, Liberty, and salvation for man, without which this race of ours is a hopeless and abandoned wreck. And when Luther gave forth his German Bible, it was not only a transcendent literary achievement, which created and fixed the classic forms of his country's language,[15] but an act of supremest wisdom and devotion; for the hope of the world is for ever cabled to the free and open Word of God.

Note:

[15] Chevalier Bunsen says; "It is Luther's genius applied to the Bible which has preserved the only unity which is, in our days, remaining to the German nation-- that of language, literature, and thought. There is no similar instance in the known history of the world of a single man achieving such a work."

LUTHER'S CONSERVATISM.

Up to the time of Luther's residence in the Wartburg nothing had been done toward changing the outward forms, ceremonies, and organization of the Church. The great thing with him had been to get the inward, central doctrine right, believing that all else would then naturally come right in due time. But while he was hidden and silent certain fanatics thrust themselves into this field, and were on the eve of precipitating everything to destruction. Tidings of the violent revolutionary spirit which had broken out reached him in his retreat and stirred him with sorrowful indignation, for it was the most damaging blow inflicted on the Reformation.

It is hard for men to keep their footing amid deep and vast commotions and not drift into ruinous excesses. Storch, and Muenzer, and Carlstadt, and Melanchthon himself, were dangerously affected by the whirl of things. Even good men sometimes forget that society cannot be conserved by mere negations; that wild and lawless revolution can never work a wholesome and abiding reformation; that the perpetuity of the Church is an historic chain, each new link of which depends on those which have gone before.

There was precious gold in the old conglomerate, which needed to be discriminated, extracted, and preserved. The divine foundations were not to be confounded with the rubbish heaped upon them. There was still a Church of Christ under the hierarchy, although the hierarchy was no part of its life or essence. The Zwickau prophets, with their new revelations and revolts against civil authority; the Wittenberg iconoclasts, with their repudiation of study and learning and all proper church order; and the Sacramentarians, with their insidious rationalism against the plain Word,--were not to be entrusted with the momentous interests with which the cause of the Reformation was freighted. And hence, at the risk of the Elector's displeasure and at the peril of his life, Luther came forth from his covert to withstand the violence which was putting everything in jeopardy.

Grandly also did he reason out the genuine Gospel principles against all these parties. He comprehended his ground from centre to circumference, and he held it alike against erring friends and menacing foes. The swollen torrent of events never once obscured his prophetic insight, never disturbed the balance of his judgment, never shook his hold upon the right. With a master-power he held revolutions and wars in check, while he revised and purified the Liturgy and Order of the Church, wrought out the evangelic truth in its applications to existing things, and reared the renewed habilitation of the pure Word and sacraments.

GROWTH OF THE REFORMATION.

It was now that Pope Leo died. His glory lasted but eight years. His successor, Adrian VI., was a moderate man, of good intentions, though he could not see what evil there was in indulgences. He exhorted Germany to get rid of Luther, but said the Church must be reformed, that the Holy See had been for years horribly polluted, and that the evils had affected head and members. He was in solemn earnest this time, and began to change and purify the papal court. To some this was as if the voice of Luther were being echoed from St. Peter's chair, and Adrian suddenly died, no man knows of what,[16] and Clement VII., a relative of Leo X., was put upon the papal throne.

In 1524 a Diet was convened at Nuremberg with reference to these same matters. Campeggio, the pope's legate, thought it prudent to make his way thither without letting himself be known, and wrote back to his master that he had to be very cautious, as the majority of the Diet consisted of "great Lutherans." At this Diet the Edict of Worms was virtually annulled, and it was plain enough that "great Lutherans" had become very numerous and powerful.

Luther himself had become of sufficient consequence for Henry VIII., king of England, to write a book against him, for which the pope gave him the title of "Defender of the Faith," and for which Luther repaid him in his own coin. Erasmus also, long the prince of the whole literary world, was dogged into the writing of a book against the great Reformer. Poor Erasmus found his match, and was overwhelmed with the result. He afterward sadly wrote: "My troops of friends are turned to enemies. Everywhere scandal pursues me and calumny denies my name. Every goose now hisses at Erasmus."

In 1525, Luther's friend and protector, the Elector Frederick, died. This would have been a sad blow for the Reformation had there been no one of like mind to take his place. But God had the man in readiness. "Frederick the Wise" was succeeded by his brother, "John the Constant."

In Hesse, in Holland, in Scandinavia, in Prussia, in Poland, in Switzerland, in France, *everywhere*, the Reformation advanced. Duke George of Saxony raged, got up an alliance against the growing cause, and beheaded citizens of Leipsic for having Luther's writings in their houses. Eck still howled from Ingolstadt for fire and fagots. The dukes of Bavaria were fierce with persecutions. The archbishop of Mayence punished cities because they would not have his priests for pastors. The emperor from Spain announced his purpose to crush and exterminate "the wickedness of Lutheranism." But it was all in vain. The sun had risen, the new era had come!

Luther now issued his ***Catechisms***, which proved a great and glorious aid to the true Gospel. Henceforth the children were to be bred up in the pure faith. Matthesius says: "If Luther in his lifetime had achieved no other work but that of bringing his two Catechisms into use, the whole world could not sufficiently thank and repay him."

A quarrel between the emperor and the pope also contributed to the progress of the Reformation. A Diet at Spire in 1526 had interposed a check to the persecuting spirit of the Romanists, and granted toleration to those of Luther's mind in all the states where his doctrines were approved. The respite lasted for three years, until Charles and Clement composed their difference and united to wreak their wrath upon Luther and his adherents.

Note:

[16] The death of Adrian VI., on the 14th of September, 1523, was a subject of general rejoicing in Rome. There was a crown of flowers hung to the door of his physician, with a card appended which read, "*To the savior of his country*."

PROTESTANTS AND WAR.

A second Diet at Spire, in 1529, revoked the former act of toleration, and demanded of all the princes and estates an unconditional surrender to the pope's decrees. This called forth the heroic **Protest** of those who stood with Luther. They refused to submit, claiming that in matters of divine service and the soul's salvation conscience and God must be obeyed rather than earthly powers. It was from this that the name of **Protestants** originated--a name which half the world now honors and accepts.

The signers of this Protest also pledged to each other their mutual support in defending their position. Zwingli urged them to make war upon the emperor. He himself afterward took the sword, and perished by it. Calvin, Cranmer, Knox, and even the Puritan Fathers as far as they had power and occasion, resorted to physical force and the civil arm to punish the rejecters of their creed. Luther repudiated all such coercion. The sword was at his command, but he opposed its use for any purposes of religion. All the weight of his great influence was given to prevent his friends from mixing external force with what should ever have its seat only in the calm conviction of the soul. He thus practically anticipated Roger Williams and William Penn and the most lauded results of modern freedom--not from constraint of circumstances and personal interests, but from his own clear insight into Gospel principles. Bloody religious wars came after he was dead, the prospect of which filled his soul with horror, and to which he could hardly give consent even in case of direst necessity for self-defence; but it is a transcendent fact that while he lived they were held in abeyance, most of all by his prayers and endeavors. He fought, indeed, as few men ever fought, but the only sword he wielded was "the sword of the Spirit, which is the Word of God."

THE CONFESSION OF AUGSBURG.

And yet another Imperial Diet was convened with reference to these religious disturbances. It was held in Augsburg in the spring of 1530. The emperor was in the zenith of his power. He had overcome his French rival. He had spoiled Rome, humbled the pope, and reorganized Italy. The Turks had withdrawn their armies. And the only thing in the way of a consolidated empire was the Reformation in Germany. To crush this was now his avowed purpose, and he anticipated no great hardship in doing it. He entered Augsburg with unwonted magnificence and pomp. He had spoken very graciously in his invitation to the princes, but it was in his heart to compel their submission to his former Edict of Worms. It behoved them to be prepared to make a full exhibit of their principles, giving the ultimatum on which they proposed to stand.

Luther had been formulating articles embodying the points adhered to in his reformatory teachings. He had prepared one set for the Marburg Conference with the Swiss divines. He had revised and elaborated these into the Seventeen Articles of Schwabach. He had also prepared another series on abuses, submitted to the Elector John at Torgau. All these were now committed to Melanchthon for careful elaboration into complete style and harmony for use at the Diet. Luther assisted in this work up to the time when the Diet convened, and what remained to be done was completed in Augsburg by Melanchthon and the Lutheran divines present with him. Luther himself could not be there, as he was a dead man to the law, and by command of his prince was detained at Coburg while the Diet was in session.

The first act of the emperor was to summon the protesting princes before him, asking of them the withdrawal of their Protest. This they refused. They felt that they had constitutional right, founded on the decision of Spire, to resist the emperor's demand; and they did not intend to surrender the just principles put forth in their noble Protest. They celebrated divine service in their quarters, led by their own clergy, and refused to join in the procession at the Roman festival of Corpus Christi. This gave much offence, and for the sake of peace they discontinued their services during the Diet.

At length they were asked to make their doctrinal presentation. Melanchthon had admirably performed the work assigned him in the making up of the Confession, and on the 25th day of June, 1530, the document, duly signed, was read aloud to the emperor in the hearing of many.

The effect of it upon the assembly was indescribable. Many of the prejudices and false notions against the Reformers were effectually dissipated. The enemies of the Reformation felt that they had solemn realities to deal with which they had never imagined. Others said that this was a more effectual preaching than that which had been suppressed. "Christ is in the Diet," said Justus Jonas, "and he does not keep silence. God's Word cannot be bound." In a word, the world now had added to it one of its greatest treasures--the renowned and imperishable AUGS-BURG CONFESSION.

Luther was eager for tidings of what transpired at the Diet. And when the Confession came, as signed and delivered, he wrote: "I thrill with joy that I have lived to see the hour in which Christ is preached by so many confessors to an assembly so illustrious in a form so beautiful."

Even Reformed authors, from Calvin down, have cheerfully added their testimony to the worth and excellence of this magnificent Confession--the first since the Athanasian Creed. A late writer of this class says of it that "it best exhibits the prevailing genius of the German Reformation, and will ever be cherished as one of the noblest monuments of faith from the pentecostal period of Protestantism."

The Romanists attempted to answer the noble Confession, but would not make their Confutation public. Compromises were proposed, but they came to naught. The Imperial troops were called into the city and the gates closed to intimidate the princes, but it resulted in greater alarm to the Romanists than to them. The confessors had taken their stand, and they were not to be moved from it. The Diet ended with the decision that they should have until the following spring to determine whether they would submit to the Roman Church or not, and, if not, that measures would then be taken for their extermination.

THE LEAGUE OF SMALCALD.

The emperor's edict appeared November 19th, and the Protestant princes at once proceeded to form a league for mutual protection against attempts to force their consciences in these sacred matters. It was with difficulty that the consent of Luther could be obtained for what, to him, looked like an arrangement to support the Gospel by the sword. But he yielded to a necessity forced by the intolerance of Rome. A convention was held at Smalcald at Christmas, 1530, and there was formed the *League of Smalcald*, which planted the political foundations of Religious Liberty for our modern world.

By the presentation of the great Confession of Augsburg, along with the formation of the League of Smalcald, the cause of Luther became embodied in the official life of nations, and the new era of Freedom had come safely to its birth. Long and terrible storms were yet to be passed, but the ship was launched which no thunders of emperors or popes could ever shatter.[17]

When the months of probation ended, France had again become troublesome to the emperor, and the Turks were renewing their movements against his dominions. He also found that he could not count on the Catholic princes for the violent suppression of the Protestants. Luther's doctrines had taken too deep hold upon their subjects to render it safe to join in a war of extermination against them.

The Zwinglians also coalesced with the Lutherans in presenting a united front against the threatened bloody coercion. The Smalcald League, moreover, had grown to be a power which even the emperor could not despise. He therefore resolved to come to terms with the Protestant members of his empire, and a peace--at least a truce--was concluded at Nuremberg, which left things as they were to wait until a general council should settle the questions in dispute.

Note:

[17] "The Reformation of Luther kindled up the minds of men afresh, leading to new habits of thought and awakening in individuals energies before unknown to themselves. The religious controversies of this period changed society, as well as religion, and to a considerable extent, where they did not change the religion of the state, they changed man himself in his modes of thought, his consciousness of his own powers, and his desire of intellectual attainment. The spirit of commercial and foreign adventure on the one hand and, on the other the assertion and maintenance of religious liberty, having their source in the Reformation, and this love of religious liberty drawing after it or bringing along with it, as it always does, an ardent devotion to the principle of civil liberty also, were the powerful influences under which character was formed and men trained for the great work of introducing English civilization, English law, and, what is more than all, Anglo-Saxon blood, into the wilderness of North America."--Daniel Webster, **Works**, vol. i. p. 94.

LUTHER'S LATER YEARS.

Luther lived nearly fifteen years after this grand crowning of his testimony, diligently laboring for Christ and his country. The most brilliant part of his career was over, but his labors still were great and important. Indeed, his whole life was intensely laborious. He was a busier man than the First Napoleon. His publications, as reckoned up by Seckendorf, amount to eleven hundred and thirty-seven. Large and small together, they number seven hundred and fifteen volumes--one for every two weeks that he lived after issuing the first. Even in the last six weeks of his life he issued thirty-one publications--more than five per week. If he had had no other cares and duties but to occupy himself with his pen, this would still prove him a very Hercules in authorship.[18]

But his later years were saddened by many anxieties, afflictions, and trials. Under God, he had achieved a transcendent work, and his confidence in its necessity, divinity, and perpetuity never failed; but he was much distressed to see it marred and damaged, as it was, by the weaknesses and passions of men.

His great influence created jealousies. His persistent conservatism gave offence. Those on whom he most relied betimes imperiled his cause by undue concessions and pusillanimity. The friends of the Reformation often looked more to political than Christian ends, or were more carnal than spiritual. Threatening civil commotions troubled him. Ultra reform attacked and blamed him. The agitations about a general council, which Rome now treacherously urged, and meant to pack for its own purposes, gave him much anxiety. It was with reference to such a council that one other great document-- *The Articles of Smalcald*--issued from his pen, in which he defined the true and final Protestant position with regard to the hierarchy, and the fundamental organization of the Church of Christ. His bodily ailments also became frequent and severe.

Prematurely old, and worn out with cares, labors, and vexations--the common lot of great heroes and benefactors--he began to long for the heavenly rest. "I am weary of the world," said he, "and it is time the world were weary of me. The parting will be easy, like a traveler leaving his inn."

He lived to his sixty-third year, and peacefully died in the faith he so effectually preached, while on a mission of reconciliation at the place where he was born, honored and lamented in his death as few men have ever been. His remains repose in front of the chancel in the castle church of Wittenberg, on the door of which his own hand had nailed the Ninety-five Theses.[19]

Note:

[18] "Never before was the human mind more prolific." "Luther holds a high and glorious place in German literature." "In his manuscripts we nowhere discover

the traces of fatigue or irritation, no embarrassment or erasures, no ill-applied epithet or unmanageable expression; and by the correctness of his writing we might imagine he was the copyist rather than the writer of the work."--So says **Audin**, his Roman Catholic biographer.

Hallam's flippant and disparaging remarks on Luther, contained in his **Introduction to the Literature of Europe**, are simply outrageous, "stupid and senseless paragraphs," evidencing a presumption on the part of their author which deserves intensest rebuke. "Hallam knows nothing about Luther; he himself confesses his inability to read him in his native German; and this alone renders him incapable of judging intelligently respecting his merits as a writer; and, knowing nothing, it would have been honorable in him to say nothing, at least to say nothing disparagingly. And, by the way, it seems to us that writing a history of European literature without a knowledge of German is much like writing a history of metals without knowing anything of iron and steel.... Luther's language became, through his writings, and has ever since remained, the language of literature and general intercourse among educated men, and is that which is now understood universally to be meant when **the German** is spoken of. His translation of the Bible is still as much the standard of purity for that language as Homer is for the Greek."--**Dr. Calvin E. Stowe.**

[19] "Nothing can be more edifying than the scene presented by the last days of Luther, of which we have the most authentic and detailed accounts. When dying he collected his last strength and offered up the following prayer: 'Heavenly Father, eternal, merciful God, thou hast revealed to me thy dear Son, our Lord Jesus Christ. Him I have taught, him I have confessed, him I love as my Saviour and Redeemer, whom the wicked persecute, dishonor, and reprove. Take my poor soul up to thee!'

"Then two of his friends put to him the solemn question: 'Reverend Father, do you die in Christ and in the doctrine you have constantly preached?' He answered by an audible and joyful '**Yes**;' and, repeating the verse, 'Father, into thy hands I commend my spirit,' he expired peacefully, without a struggle."--**Encyc. Britannica.**

PERSONALE OF LUTHER.

The personal appearance of this extraordinary man is but poorly given in the painted portraits of him. Written descriptions inform us that he was of medium size, handsomely proportioned, and somewhat darkly complected. His arched brows, high cheek-bones, and powerful jaws and chin gave to his face an outline of rug-gedness; but his features were regular, and softened all over with benevolence and every refined feeling. He had remarkable eyes, large, full, deep, dark, and brilliant, with a sort of amber circle around the pupil, which made them seem to emit fire when under excitement. His hair was dark and waving, but became entirely white in his later years. His mouth was elegantly formed, expressive of determination, tenderness, affection, and humor. His countenance was elevated, open, brave, and unflinching. His neck was short and strong and his breast broad and full.

Though compactly built, he was generally spare and wasted from incessant studies, hard labor, and an abstemious life.

Mosellanus, the moderator at the Leipsic Disputation, describes him quite fully as he appeared at that time, and says that "his body was so reduced by cares and study that one could almost count his bones." He himself makes frequent allusion to his wasted and enfeebled body. His health was never robust. He was a small eater. Melanchthon says: "I have seen him, when he was in full health, absolutely neither eat nor drink for four days together. At other times I have seen him, for many days, content with the slightest allowance, a salt herring and a small hunch of bread per day."

Mosellanus further says that his manners were cultured and friendly, with nothing of stoical severity or pride in him--that he was cheerful and full of wit in company, and at all times fresh, joyous, inspiring, and pleasant.

Honest naturalness, grand simplicity, and an unpretentious majesty of charac-ter breathed all about him. An indwelling vehemency, a powerful will, and a firm confidence could readily be seen, but calm and mellowed with generous kindness, without a trace of selfishness or vanity. He was jovial, free-spoken, open, easily ap-proached, and at home with all classes.

Audin says of him that "his voice was clear and sonorous, his eye beaming with fire, his head of the antique cast, his hands beautiful, and his gesture graceful and abounding--at once Rabelais and Fontaine, with the droll humor of the one and the polished elegance of the other."

In society and in his home he was genial, playful, instructive, and often bril-liant. His *Table-Talk*, collected (not always judiciously) by his friends, is one of the most original and remarkable of productions. He loved children and young people, and brought up several in his house besides his own. He had an inexhaustible flow of ready wit and good-humor, prepared for everybody on all occasions. He was a frank and free correspondent, and let out his heart in his letters, six large volumes of which have been preserved.

He was specially fond of music, and cultivated it to a high degree. He could sing and play like a woman.[20] "I have no pleasure in any man," said he, "who despises music. It is no invention of ours; it is the gift of God. I place it next to theology."

He was himself a great musician and hymnist. Handel confesses that he derived singular advantage from the study of his music; and Coleridge says: "He did as much for the Reformation by his hymns as by his translation of the Bible." To this day he is the chief singer in a Church of pre-eminent song. Heine speaks of "those stirring songs which escaped from him in the very midst of his combats and necessities, like flowers making their way from between rough stones or moonbeams glittering among dark clouds." *Ein feste Burg* welled from his great heart like the gushing of the waters from the smitten rock of Horeb to inspirit and refresh God's faint and doubting people as long as the Church is in this earthly wilderness. There is a mighty soul in it which lifts one, as on eagles' wings, high and triumphant over the blackest storms. And his whole life was a brilliantly enacted epic of marvelous grandeur and pathos.[21]

Note:

[20] Mattaehus Ratzenberger, in a passage of his biography preserved in the *Bibliotheca Ducalis Gothana*, says: "Lutherus had also this custom: as soon as he had eaten the evening meal with his table companions he would fetch out of his little writing-room his *partes* and hold a *musicam* with those of them who had a mind for music. Greatly was he delighted when a good composition of the old master fitted the responses or *hymnos de tempore anni*, and especially did he enjoy the *cantu Gregoriana* and chorale. But if at times he perceived in a new song that it was incorrectly copied he set it again upon the lines (that is, he brought the parts together and rectified it *in continenti*). Right gladly did he join in the singing when *hymnus* or *responsorium de tempore* had been set by the *Musicus* to a *Cantum Gregorianum*, as we have said, and his young sons, Martinus and Paulus, had also after table to sing the *responsoria de tempore*, as at Christmas, *Ver-*

bum caro factum est, *In principio erat verbum*; at Easter, **Christus resurgens ex mortuis**, *Vita sanctorum*, *Victimae paschali laudes*, etc. In these **responsoria** he always sang along with his sons, and in **cantu figurali** he sang the alto."

The alto which Luther sang must not be confounded with the alto part of to-day. Here it means the **cantus firmus**, the melody around which the old composers wove their contrapuntal ornamentation.

Luther was the creator of German congregational singing.

[21] Luther's first poetic publication seems to have been certain verses composed on the martyrdom of two young Christian monks, who were burned alive at Brussels in 1523 for their faithful confession of the evangelical doctrines. A translation of a part of this composition is given in D'Aubigne's **History of the Reformation** in these beautiful and stirring words:

"Flung to the heedless winds or on the waters cast,
Their ashes shall be watched, and gathered at the last;
And from that scattered dust, around us and abroad,
Shall spring a plenteous seed of witnesses for God.

"Jesus hath now received their latest living breath,
Yet vain is Satan's boast of victory in their death.
Still, still, though dead, they speak, and trumpet-tongued proclaim
To many a wakening land the One availing Name."

Audin, though a Romanist, says: "The hymns which he translated from the Latin into German may be unreservedly praised, as also those which he composed for the members of his own communion. He did not travesty the sacred Word nor set his anger to music. He is grave, simple, solemn, and grand. He was at once the poet and musician of a great number of his hymns."

HIS GREAT QUALITIES.

Luther's qualities of mind, heart, and attainment were transcendent. Though naturally meek and diffident, when it came to matters of duty and conviction he was courageous, self-sacrificing, and brave beyond any mere man known to history. Elijah fled before the threats of Jezebel, but no powers on earth could daunt the soul of Luther. Even the apparitions of the devil himself could not disconcert him.

Roman Catholic authors agree that "Nature gave him a German industry and strength and an Italian spirit and vivacity," and that "nobody excelled him in philosophy and theology, and nobody equaled him in eloquence."

His mental range was not confined to any one set of subjects. In the midst of his profound occupation with questions of divinity and the Church "his mind was literally world-wide. His eyes were for ever observant of what was around him. At a time when science was hardly out of its shell he had observed Nature with the liveliest curiosity. He studied human nature like a dramatist. Shakespeare himself drew from him. His memory was a museum of historical information, anecdotes of great men, and old German literature, songs, and proverbs, to the latter of which he made many rich additions from his own genius. Scarce a subject could be spoken of on which he had not thought and on which he had not something remarkable to say."[22] In consultations upon public affairs, when the most important things hung in peril, his contemporaries speak with amazement of the gigantic strength of his mind, the unexampled acuteness of his intellect, the breadth and loftiness of his understanding and counsels.

But, though so great a genius, he laid great stress on sound and thorough learning and study. "The strength and glory of a town," said he, "does not depend on its wealth, its walls, its great mansions, its powerful armaments, but in the number of its learned, serious, kind, and well-educated citizens." He was himself a great scholar, far beyond what we would suspect in so perturbed a life, or what he cared to parade in his writings. He mastered the ancient languages, and insisted on the perpetual study of them as "the scabbard which holds the sword of the Spirit, the cases which enclose the precious jewels, the vessels which contain the old wine, the baskets which carry the loaves and the fishes for the feeding of the multitude." His associates say of him that he was a great reader, eagerly perusing the Church Fathers, old and new, and all histories, well retaining what he read, and using the same with great skill as occasion called.

Melanchthon, who knew him well, and knew well how to judge of men's powers and attainments, said of him: "He is too great, too wonderful, for me to describe. Whatever he writes, whatever he utters, goes to the soul and fixes itself like arrows in the heart. ***He is a miracle among men.***"

Nor was he without the humility of true greatness. Newton's comparison of himself to a child gathering shells and pebbles on the shore, while the great ocean of truth lay all undiscovered before him, has been much cited and lauded as an illustration of the modesty of true science. But long before Newton had Luther said of himself, in the midst of his mighty achievements, "Only a little of the first fruits of wisdom--only a few fragments of the boundless heights, breadths, and depths of truth--have I been able to gather."

He was a man of amazing *faith*--that mighty principle which looks at things invisible, joins the soul to divine Omnipotence, and launches out unfalteringly upon eternal realities, and which is ever the chief factor in all God's heroes of every age. He dwelt in constant nearness and communion with the Eternal Spirit, which reigns in the heavens and raises the willing and obedient into blessed instruments of itself for the actualizing of ends and ideals beyond and above the common course of things. With his feet ever planted on the promises, he could lay his hands upon the Throne, and thus was lifted into a sublimity of energy, endurance, and command which made him one of the phenomenal wonders of humanity. He was a very Samson in spiritual vigor, and another Hannah's son in the strength and victory of his prayers.

Dr. Calvin E. Stowe says: "There was probably never created a more powerful human being, a more gigantic, full-proportioned MAN, in the highest sense of the term. All that belongs to human nature, all that goes to constitute a MAN, had a strongly-marked development in him. He was a *model man*, one that might be shown to other beings in other parts of the universe as a specimen of collective manhood in its maturest growth."

As the guide and master of one of the greatest revolutions of time we look in vain for any one with whom to compare him, and as a revolutionary orator and preacher he had no equal. Richter says, "His words are half-battles." Melanchthon likens them to thunderbolts. He was at once a Peter and a Paul, a Socrates and an AEsop, a Chrysostom and a Savonarola, a Shakespeare and a Whitefield, all condensed in one.

Note:

[22] Froude supplemented.

HIS ALLEGED COARSENESS.

Some blame him for not using kid gloves in handling the ferocious bulls, bears, and he-goats with whom he had to do. But what, otherwise, would have become of the Reformation? His age was savage, and the men he had to meet were savage, and the matters at stake touched the very life of the world. What would a Chesterfield or an Addison have been in such a contest? Erasmus said he had horns, and knew how to use them, but that Germany needed just such a master. He understood the situation. "These gnarled logs," said he, "will not split without iron wedges and heavy malls. The air will not clear without lightning and thunder."[23]

But if he was rough betimes, he could be as gentle and tender as a maiden, and true to himself in both. He could fight monsters all day, and in the evening take his lute, gaze at the stars, sing psalms, and muse upon the clouds, the fields, the flowers, the birds, dissolved in melody and devotion. Feared by the mighty of the earth, the dictator and reprimander of kings, the children loved him, and his great heart was as playful among them as one of themselves. If he was harsh and unsparing upon hypocrites, malignants, and fools, he called things by their right names, and still was as loving as he was brave. Since King David's lament over Absalom no more tender or pathetic scene has appeared in history or in fiction than his outpouring of paternal love and grief over the deathbed, coffin, and grave of his young and precious daughter Madeleine. "I know of few things more touching," says Carlyle, "than those soft breathings of affection, soft as a child's or a mother's, in this great wild heart of Luther;" and adds: "I will call this Luther a true Great Man; great in intellect, in courage, affection, and integrity; one of our most lovable and precious men. Great not as a hewn obelisk, but as an Alpine mountain, so simple, honest, spontaneous; not setting up to be great at all; there for quite another purpose than being great. Ah, yes, unsubduable granite, piercing far and wide into the Heavens; yet, in the clefts of it, fountains, green, beautiful valleys with flowers. A right Spiritual Hero and Prophet; once more, a true Son of Nature and Fact, for whom these centuries, and many that are yet to come, will be thankful to Heaven."

Note:

[23] "It must be observed that the coarse vituperations which shock the reader in Luther's controversial works were not peculiar to him, being commonly used by scholars and divines of the Middle Ages in their disputations. The invectives

of Valla, Filelfo, Poggio, and other distinguished scholars against each other are notorious; and this bad taste continued in practice long after Luther down to the seventeenth century, and traces of it are found in writers of the eighteenth, even in some of the works of the polished and courtly Voltaire."--*Cyclopaedia of Soc. for Diffus. of Useful Knowledge.*

HIS MARVELOUS ACHIEVEMENTS.

A lone man, whose days were spent in poverty; who could withstand the mighty Vatican and all its flaming Bulls; whose influence evoked and swayed successive Diets of the empire; whom repeated edicts from the Imperial throne could not crush; whom the talent, eloquence, and towering authority of the Roman hierarchy assailed in vain; whom the attacks of kings of state and kings of literature could not disable; to offset whose opinions the greatest general council the Church of Rome ever held had to be convened, and, after sitting eighteen years, could not adjourn without conceding much to his positions; and whose name the greatest and most enlightened nations of the earth hail with glad acclaim,--necessarily must have been a wonder of a man.[24]

To begin with a minority consisting of one, and conquer kingdoms with the mere sword of his mouth; to bear the anathemas of Church and the ban of empire, and triumph in spite of them; to refuse to fall down before the golden image of the combined Nebuchadnezzars of his time, though threatened with the burning fires of earth and hell; to turn iconoclast of such magnitude and daring as to think of smiting the thing to pieces in the face of principalities and powers to whom it was as God--nay, to attempt this, ***and to succeed in it***,--here was sublimity of heroism and achievement explainable only in the will and providence of the Almighty, set to recover His Gospel to a perishing race.[25]

Note:

[24] "In no other instance have such great events depended upon the courage, sagacity, and energy of a single man, who, by his sole and unassisted efforts, made his solitary cell the heart and centre of the most wonderful and important commotion the world ever witnessed--who by the native force and vigor of his genius attacked and successfully resisted, and at length overthrew, the most awful and sacred authority that ever imposed its commands on mankind."--A letter prefixed to Luther's ***Table-Talk*** in the folio edition of 1652.

[25] "To overturn a system of religious belief founded on ancient and deep-rooted prejudices, supported by power and defended with no less art than industry--to establish in its room doctrines of the most contrary genius and tendency, and to accomplish all this, not by external violence or the force of arms, are operations which historians the least prone to credulity and superstition ascribe to that divine providence which with infinite ease can bring about events which to human sagacity appear impossible."--Robertson's ***Charles V.***

HIS IMPRESS UPON THE WORLD.

To describe the fruits of Luther's labors would require the writing of the whole history of modern civilization and the setting forth of the noblest characteristics of this our modern world.[26]

On the German nation he has left more of his impress than any other man has left on any nation. The German people love to speak of him as the creative master of their noble language and literature, the great prophet and glory of their country. There is nothing so consecrated in all his native land as the places which connect with his life, presence, and deeds.

But his mighty impress is not confined to Germany. "He grasped the iron trumpet of his mother-tongue and blew a blast that shook the nations from Rome to the Orkneys." He is not only the central figure of Germany, but of Europe and of the whole modern world. Take Luther away, with the fruits of his life and deeds, and man to-day would cease to be what he is.

Frederick von Schlegel, though a Romanist, affirms that "it was upon him and his soul that the fate of Europe depended." And on the fate of Europe then depended the fate of our race.

Michelet, also a Romanist, pronounces Luther "the restorer of liberty in modern times;" and adds: "If we at this day exercise in all its plenitude the first and highest privilege of human intelligence, it is to him we are indebted for it."

"And that any faith," says Froude, "any piety, is alive now, even in the Roman Church itself, whose insolent hypocrisy he humbled into shame, is due in large measure to the poor miner's son."

He certainly is to-day the most potently living man who has lived this side of the Middle Ages. The pulsations of his great heart are felt through the whole ***corpus*** of our civilization.

"Four potentates," says the late Dr. Krauth, "ruled the mind of Europe in the Reformation: the emperor, Erasmus, the pope, and Luther. The pope wanes; Erasmus is little; the emperor is nothing; but Luther abides as a power for all time. His image casts itself upon the current of ages as the mountain mirrors itself in the river which winds at its foot. He has monuments in marble and bronze, and medals in silver and gold, but his noblest monument is the best love of the best hearts, and the brightest and purest impression of his image has been left in the souls of regenerated nations."

Many and glowing are the eulogies which have been pronounced upon him, but Frederick von Schlegel, speaking from the side of Rome, gives it as his conviction that "few, even of his own disciples, appreciate him highly enough." Genius, learning, eloquence, and song have volunteered their noble efforts to do him justice; centuries have added their light and testimony; half the world in its enthusiasm has urged on the inspiration; but the story in its full dimensions has not yet been adequately told. The skill and energy of other generations will yet be taxed to give it, if, indeed, it ever can be given apart from the illuminations of eternity.[27]

Note:

[26] "From the commencement of the religious war in Germany to the Peace of Westphalia scarce anything great or memorable occurred in the European political world with which the Reformation was not essentially connected. Every event in the history of the world in this interval, if not directly occasioned, was nearly affected, by this religious revolution, and every state, great or small, remotely or immediately felt its influence."--Schiller's ***Thirty Years' War***, vol. i. p. 1.

[27] "Luther was as wonderful as he was great. His personal experience in divine things was as deep as his mind was mighty, large, and unbounded. Though called by the Most High, and continued by his appointment, in the midst of papal darkness, idolatry, and error, with no companions but the saints of the Bible, nor any other light but the lamp of the Word to guide his feet, his heaven-taught soul was ministerially furnished with as rich pasture for the sheep of Christ, as awful ammunition for the terror and destruction of the enemies by which he and they were perpetually surrounded. The sphere of his mighty ministry was not bounded by his defence of the truth against the great and powerful. No! He was as rich a pastor, as terrible a warrior. He fed the sheep in the fattest pastures, while he destroyed the

wolves on every side. Nor will those pastures be dried up or lost until time, nations, and the churches of God shall be no more."--Dr. Cole's ***Pref. to Luther on Genesis***.

HIS ENEMIES AND REVILERS.

Rome has never forgotten nor forgiven him. She sought his life while living, and she curses him in his grave. Profited by his labors beyond what she ever could have been without him, she strains and chokes with anathemas upon his name and everything that savors of him. Her children are taught from infancy to hate and abhor him as they hope for salvation. Many are the false turns and garbled forms in which her writers hold up his words and deeds to revenge themselves on his memory. Again and again the oft-answered and exploded calumnies are revived afresh to throw dishonor on his cause. Even while the free peoples of the earth are making these grateful acknowledgments of the priceless boon that has come to them through his life and labors, press and platform hiss with stale vituperations from the old enemy. And a puling Churchism outside of Rome takes an ill pleasure in following after her to gather and retail this vomit of malignity.

Luther was but a man. No one claims that he was perfection. But if those who sought his destruction while he lived had had no greater faults than he, with better grace their modern representatives might indulge their genius for his defamation. At best, as we might suppose, it is the little men, the men of narrow range and nar-row heart--men dwarfed by egotism, bigotry, and self-conceit--who see the most of these defects. Nobler minds, contemplating him from loftier standpoints, observe but little of them, and even honor them above the excellencies of common men. "The proofs that he was in some things like other men," says Lessing, "are to me as precious as the most dazzling of his virtues."[28]

And, with all, where is the gain or wisdom of blowing smoke upon a diamond? The sun itself has holes in it too large for half a dozen worlds like ours to fill, but wherein is that great luminary thereby unfitted to be the matchless centre of our system, the glorious source of day, and the sublime symbol of the Son of God?

If Luther married a beautiful woman, the proofs of which do not appear, it is what every other honest man would do if it suited him and he were free to do it.

If he broke his vows to get a wife, of which there is no evidence, when vows are taken by mistake, tending to dishonor God, work unrighteousness, and hinder virtuous example and proper life, they ought to be broken, the sooner the better.

And, whatever else may be alleged to his discredit, and whoever may arise to heap scandal on his name, the grand facts remain that it was chiefly through his marvelous qualities, word, and work that the towering dominion of the Papacy was humbled and broken for ever; that prophets and apostles were released from their prisons once more to preach and prophesy to men; that the Church of the early times was restored to the bereaved world; that the human mind was set free to read and follow God's Word for itself; that the masses of neglected and downtrodden humanity were made into populations of live and thinking beings; and that the nations of the earth have become repossessed of their "inalienable rights" of "life, liberty, and the pursuit of happiness."

> "And let the pope and priests their victor scorn,
> Each fault reveal, each imperfection scan,
> And by their fell anatomy of hate
> His life dissect with satire's keenest edge;
> Yet still may Luther, with his mighty heart,
> Defy their malice.
> Far beyond *them* soars the soul
> They slander. From his tomb there still comes forth
> A magic which appalls them by its power;
> And the brave monk who made the Popedom rock
> Champions a world to show his equal yet!"

Note:

[28] "It was by some of these qualities which we are now apt to blame that Luther was fitted for accomplishing the great work which he undertook. To rouse mankind when sunk in ignorance and superstition, and to encounter the rage of bigotry armed with power, required the utmost vehemence of zeal as well as temper daring to excess."--Robertson's *Charles V.*

THE FOUNDING OF PENNSYLVANIA.

I. THE HISTORY AND THE MEN.

It was in 1492, just nine years after Luther's birth, that the intrepid Genoese, Christopher Columbus, under the patronage of Ferdinand, king of Spain, made the discovery of land on this side of the Atlantic Ocean. A few years later the distinguished Florentine, Americus Vespucius, set foot on its more interior coasts, described their features, and imprinted his name on this Western Continent. But it was not until more than a century later that permanent settlements of civilized people upon these shores began to be made.

During the early part of the seventeenth century several such settlements were effected. A company of English adventurers planted themselves on the banks of the James River and founded Virginia (1607). The Dutch of Holland, impelled by the spirit of mercantile enterprise, established a colony on the Hudson, and founded what afterward became the city and State of New York (1614). Then a shipload of English Puritans, flying from religious oppression, landed at Plymouth Rock and made the beginning of New England (1620). A little later Lord Baltimore founded a colony on the Chesapeake and commenced the State of Maryland (1633). But it was not until 1637-38 that the first permanent settlement was made in what subsequently became the State of Pennsylvania.

MOVEMENTS IN SWEDEN.

From the year 1611 to 1632 there was upon the throne of Sweden one of the noblest of kings, a great champion of religious liberty, the lamented and ever-to-be-remembered GUSTAVUS ADOLPHUS.

In his profound thinking to promote the glory of God and the good of men his attention rested on this vast domain of wild lands in America. He knew the sorrows and distresses which thousands all over Europe were suffering from the constant and devastating religious wars, and the purpose was kindled in his heart to plant here a colony as the beginning of a general asylum for these homeless and persecuted people, and determined to foster the same by his royal protection and care.

"To this end he sent forth letters patent, dated Stockholm, 2d of July, 1626, wherein all, both high and low, were invited to contribute something to the company according to their means. The work was completed in the Diet of the following year (1627), when the estates of the realm gave their assent and confirmed the measure. Those who took part in this company were: His Majesty's mother, the queen-dowager Christina, the Prince John Casimir, the Royal Council, the most distinguished of the nobility, the highest officers of the army, the bishops and other clergymen, together with the burgomasters and aldermen of the cities, as well as a large number of the people generally. For the management and working of the plan there were appointed an admiral, vice-admiral, chapman, under-chapman, assistants, and commissaries, also a body of soldiers duly officered."[29] And a more beneficent, brilliant, and promising arrangement of the sort was perhaps never made. The devout king intended his grand scheme "for the honor of God," for the welfare of his subjects and suffering Christians in general, and as a means "to extend the doctrines of Christ among the heathen."

But when everything was complete and in full progress to go into effect, King Gustavus Adolphus was called to join and lead the allied armies of the Protestant kingdoms of Germany against the endeavors of the papal powers to crush out the cause of evangelical Christianity and free conscience.[30]

For the ensuing five years the attention and energies of Sweden were preoccupied, first with the Polish, and then with these wars, and the colonization scheme was interrupted.

Then came the famous battle of Luetzen, 1632, bringing glorious victory over the gigantic Wallenstein, but death to the victor, the royal Adolphus.[31]

Only a few days before that dreadful battle he spoke of his colonization plan, and commended it to the German people at Nuremberg as "the jewel of his kingdom;" but with the king's death the company disbanded.

We could almost wish that Gustavus had lived to carry out his humane and magnificent proposals with reference to this colony as well as for Europe; but his work was done. What America lost by his death she more than regained in the final success and secure establishment of the holy cause for which he sacrificed his life.

Note:

[29] Acrelius's ***History***, p. 21.

[30] "When he now beheld that the cause of Protestantism was menaced more seriously than ever throughout the whole of Germany, he took the decisive step, and, formally declaring war against the emperor, he, on the 24th of June, 1630, landed on the coast of Pomerania with fifteen thousand Swedes. As soon as he stepped upon shore he dropped on his knees in prayer, while his example was followed by his whole army. Truly he had undertaken, with but small and limited means, a great and mighty enterprise." "The Swedes, so steady and strict in their discipline, appeared as protecting angels, and as the king advanced the belief spread far and near throughout the land that he was sent from heaven as its preserver."--***History of Germany***, by Kohlrausch, pp. 328, 329.

"Bavaria and the Tyrol excepted, every province throughout Germany had battled for liberty of conscience, and yet the whole of Germany, notwithstanding her universal inclination for the Reformation, had been deceived in her hopes: a second Imperial edict seemed likely to crush the few remaining privileges spared by the edict of restitution.... Gustavus, urged by his sincere piety, resolved to take up arms in defence of Protestantism and to free Germany from the yoke imposed by the Jesuits."--Menzel's ***History of Germany***, vol. ii. pp. 345, 346.

"The party of the Catholics were carrying all before them, and everything seemed to promise that Ferdinand (the Roman Catholic emperor) would become absolute through the whole of Germany, and succeed in that scheme which he seemed to meditate, of entirely abolishing the Protestant religion in the empire. But this miserable prospect, both of political and religious thraldom, was dissolved by the great Gustavus Adolphus being invited by the Protestant princes of Germany to espouse the cause of the Reformed religion, being himself of that persuasion."--Tytler's ***Univ. Hist.***, vol. ii. p. 451.

[31] The death of Gustavus Adolphus is thus described by Kohlrausch: "The king spent the cold autumnal night in his carriage, and advised with his generals about the battle. The morning dawned, and a thick fog covered the entire plain;

the troops were drawn up in battle-array, and the Swedes sang, accompanied with trumpets and drums, Luther's hymn, ***Ein feste Burg ist unser Gott*** ('A mighty fortress is our God'), together with the hymn composed by the king himself, ***Verzage nicht, du Haeuflein klein*** ('Fear not the foe, thou little flock'). Just after eleven o'clock, when the sun was emerging from behind the clouds, and after a short prayer, the king mounted his horse, placed himself at the head of the right wing-- the left being commanded by Bernard of Weimar--and cried, 'Now, onward! May our God direct us!--Lord, Lord! help me this day to fight for the glory of thy name!' and, throwing away his cuirass with the words, 'God is my shield!' he led his troops to the front of the Imperialists, who were well entrenched on the paved road which leads from Luetzen to Leipsic, and stationed in the deep trenches on either side. A deadly cannonade saluted the Swedes, and many here met their death; but their places were filled by others, who leaped over the trench, and the troops of Wallenstein retreated.

"In the mean time, Pappenheim came up with his cavalry from Halle, and the battle was renewed with the utmost fury. The Swedish infantry fled behind the trenches. To assist them, the king hastened to the spot with a company of horse, and rode in full speed considerably in advance to descry the weak points of the enemy; only a few of his attendants, and Francis, duke of Saxe-Lauenberg, rode with him. His short-sightedness led him too near a squadron of Imperial horse; he received a shot in his arm, which nearly precipitated him to the ground; and just as he was turning to be led away from the tumultuous scene he received a second shot in the back. With the exclamation, 'My God! my God!' he fell from his horse, which also was shot in the neck, and was dragged for some distance, hanging by the stirrup. The duke abandoned him, but his faithful page tried to raise him, when the Imperial horsemen shot him also, killed the king, and completely plundered him." Pappenheim was also mortally wounded, Wallenstein retreated, and the victory was with the Swedes, but their noble king was no more.

THE SWEDISH PROPOSAL.

The plan of this illustrious king was to found here upon the Delaware a free state under his sovereign protection, where the laborer should enjoy the fruit of his toil, where the rights of conscience should be preserved inviolate, and which should be open to the whole Protestant world, then and for long time engaged in bloody conflict with the papal powers for the maintenance of its existence. Here all were to be secure in their persons, their property, and their religious convictions. It was to be a place of refuge and peace for the persecuted of all nations, of security for the honor of the wives and daughters of those fleeing from sword, fire, and rapine, and from homes made desolate by oppressive war. It was to be a land of universal liberty for all classes, the soil of which was never to be burdened with slaves.[32] And in all the colonies of America there was not a more thoroughly digested system for the practical realization of these ideas than that which the great Gustavus Adolphus had thus arranged.

Nor did it altogether die with his death. His mantle fell upon one of the best and greatest of men. Axel Oxenstiern, his friend and prime minister, and his successor in the administration of the affairs of the kingdom, was as competent as he was zealous to fulfill the wise plans and ideas of the slain king, not only with reference to Sweden and Europe, but also with regard to the contemplated colony in America.

Having taken the matter into his own hands, on the 10th of April, 1633, only a few months after Gustavus's death, Oxenstiern renewed the movement which had been laid aside, and repeated the offer to Germany and other countries, inviting general co-operation in the noble enterprise.

Peter Minuit, a member of a distinguished family of Rhenish Prussia, who had been for years the able director and president of the Dutch mercantile establishment on the Hudson, presented himself in Sweden, and entered into the matter with great energy and enthusiasm. And by the end of 1637 or early in 1638 two ships were seen entering and ascending the Delaware, freighted with the elements and nucleus of the new state, such as Gustavus had projected.

These ships, under Minuit, landed their passengers but a few miles south of where Philadelphia now stands, and thus made the first beginning of what has since become the great and happy Commonwealth of Pennsylvania.

This was *six years before Penn was born*.

Note:

[32] The description of the features of this plan is taken from Geijer's *Svenska Folkets Historia*, vol. iii. p. 128, given by Dr. Reynolds in his Introduction to Israel Acrelius's *History of New Sweden*, published by the Historical Society of Pennsylvania. It was first propounded by Gustavus Adolphus in 1624. Also referred to

in *Argonautica Gustaviana*, pp. 3 and 22.

WAS PENN AWARE OF THESE PLANS?

How far William Penn was illuminated and influenced by the ideas of the great and wise Gustavus Adolphus in reference to the founding of a free state in America as an asylum for the persecuted and suffering people of God in the Old World, is nowhere told; but there is reason to believe that he knew of them, and took his own plans from them.

A few facts bearing on the point may here be noted.

One peculiarly striking is, that the same plan and principles with reference to such a colonial state which Penn brought hither in the *Welcome* in 1682 were already matured and widely propounded by the illustrious Swedish king more than half a century before they practically entered Penn's mind.

Another is, that these proposals and principles were generally promulgated throughout Europe--first by Gustavus and those associated with him in the matter, and then again by Oxenstiern, in Germany, Holland, and other countries.

Still another is, that in 1677 Penn made a special tour of three months through Holland and various parts of Germany, visiting and conferring with many of the most pious and devoted people, including distinguished men and women, and clergy and laity of high standing, information, and influence. He made considerable stay in Frankfort, where he says both Calvinists and Lutherans received him with gladness of heart. He visited Mayence, Worms, Mannheim, Mulheim, Duesseldorf, Herwerden, Embaden, Bremen, etc., etc., concerning which the editor of his *Life and Writings* says he had "interesting interviews with many persons eminent for their talents, learning, or social position." Among them were such as Elizabeth, Princess Palatine, niece of Charles I. of England and the daughter of the king of Bohemia, the special friend of Gustavus Adolphus, who died of horror on hearing that Gustavus was slain; Anna Maria, countess of Hornes; the countess and earl of Falkenstein and Brueck; the president of the council of state at Embaden; the earl of Donau, and the like; among all of which it is hardly possible that he should have failed to meet with the proposals which had gone out over all Protestant Europe from the throne of Sweden. Nor is there any evidence that William Penn had thought of founding a free Christian state in America until immediately after his return to England from this tour on the Continent.

Furthermore, the plans of Gustavus respecting his projected colony on the Delaware were well understood in official circles in England itself, especially in London, from 1634. John Oxenstiern, brother of the great chancellor, was at that time Swedish ambassador in London, and in that year he obtained from King Charles I. a renunciation and cession to Sweden of all claims of the English to the country on the Delaware growing out of the rights of first discovery, and for the very purposes of this colonial free state and asylum first projected by the Swedish king.

THE SWEDES IN ADVANCE OF PENN.

We are left to our own inferences from these facts. But, however much or little Penn may have been directly influenced and guided by what Gustavus Adolphus had conceived and elaborated on the subject, the wise and noble conception which he brought with him for practical realization in 1682 was known to the European peoples for more than fifty years before he laid hold on it. The same had also been one of the chief sources of the inspiration of Lord Baltimore in the founding of the colony of Maryland, of which Penn was not ignorant. And the same, not unknown to him, had already begun to be realized here in what is now called Pennsylvania full forty-four years before his arrival.

Shipload after shipload of sturdy and devoted people, mostly Swedes, animated with the same grand ideas, had here been landed. And so successfully had they battled with the perils and hardships of the wilderness, and so justly had they treated and arranged to dwell in peace and love with the wild inhabitants of the forests, that when Penn came he found everything prepared to his hand. The Swedes alone already numbered about one thousand strong. They had conquered the wild woods, built them homes, and opened plantations; and "the eye of the stranger could begin to gaze with interest upon the signs of public improvement, ever regularly advancing, from the region of Wilmington to that of Philadelphia."

When Penn landed he found a town and court-house at New Castle, and a town and place of public assemblage at Upland, and a Christian and free people in possession of the territory, with whom it was necessary for him to treat before his charter could avail for the planting of his colony. The land to which the Swedes had acquired title (by England's release to Sweden of all claim from right of discovery, by charter from Sweden, by purchase from the Indians, first under Minuit, the first governor, and then under his successor, Governor Printz, and by other purchases or agreements) was the west bank of the Delaware River from Cape Henlopen to Trenton Falls, and thence westward to the great fall in the Susquehanna, near the mouth of the Conewaga Creek, which included nearly the whole of Eastern Pennsylvania and Delaware.

The fortunes of war, in Europe and between the colonies, in course of time complicated the titles to one and another portion of this territory, but the Swedes and Dutch occupied and held the most prominent parts of it by right of actual possession when and after Penn's charter was granted.

PENN'S CHARTER AND ARRIVAL.

But when Penn arrived he brought with him letters patent from Charles II., king of England, to this same district of country and the wilds indefinitely beyond it, having also obtained from his friend, the king's brother, the duke of York, full releases of the claims vested in him to the "Lower Counties," which now form the State of Delaware.

Penn was accompanied by from sixty to seventy colonists--all that survived the scourge which visited them in their passage across the sea. He landed first at New Castle, of which the Dutch of New York had by conquest obtained possession. To them he made known his grants and his plans, and succeeded in securing their acquiescence in them.

Thence he came to Upland (Chester), the head-quarters of the Swedes, who "received their new fellow-citizens with great friendliness, carried up their goods and furniture from the ships, and entertained them in their own houses without charge." His proposals with regard to the establishment of a united commonwealth they also received with much favor. And immediately thereupon he convened a general assembly of the citizens, which sat for three days, by which an act was passed for the consolidation of the various interests and parties on the ground, a code of general regulations adopted, and the necessary features of a common government enacted; all of which together formed the basis of our present commonwealth.

HOW PENNSYLVANIA WAS NAMED.

The name which Penn had chosen for the territory of his grant was *Sylvania*, but the king prefixed the name of Penn and called it *Penn's* Silvania (*Penn's Woods*), in honor of the recipient's father, Sir William Penn, a distinguished officer in the British navy. Penn sought to have the title changed so as to leave his own name out, as he thought it savored too much of personal vanity; but his efforts did not avail. And thus our great old commonwealth took the name of **Pennsylvania**, and the city of Philadelphia was laid out and named by Penn himself as its capital.

THE MEN OF THOSE TIMES.

In dwelling upon the founding of our happy commonwealth it is pleasant to contemplate how enlightened and exalted were the men whom Providence employed for the performance of this important work.

Many are apt to think ours the age of culminated enlightenment, dignity, wisdom, and intelligence, and look upon the fathers of two and three hundred years ago as mere pigmies, just emerging from an era of barbarism and ignorance, not at all to be compared with the proud wiseacres of our day. Never was there a greater mistake. The shallowness and flippancy of the leaders and politicians of this last quarter of the nineteenth century show them but little more than school-boys compared with the sturdy, sober-minded, deep-principled, dignified, and grand-spirited men who discovered and opened this continent and laid the foundations of our country's greatness. And those who were most concerned in the founding of our own commonwealth suffer in no respect in comparison with the greatest and the best.

GUSTAVUS ADOLPHUS.

I have named the illustrious GUSTAVUS ADOLPHUS as the man, above all, who first conceived, sketched, and propounded the grand idea of such a state. What other colonies reached only through varied experiments and gradual developments, Pennsylvania had clear and mature, in ideal and in fact, from the very earliest beginning; and the royal heart and brain of Sweden were its source.

Gustavus Adolphus was born a prince in the regular line of Sweden's ancient kings. His grandfather, Gustavus Vasa, was a man of thorough culture, excellent ability, and sterling moral qualities. When in Germany he was an earnest listener to Luther's preaching, became his friend and correspondent, a devout confessor and patron of the evangelic faith, and the wise establisher of the Reformation in his kingdom.

Adolphus inherited all his grandfather's high qualities. He was the idol of his father, Charles IX., and was devoutly trained from earliest childhood in the evangelic faith, educated in thorough princely style, familiarized with governmental affairs from the time he was a boy, and developed into an exemplary, wise, brave, and devoted Christian man and illustrious king.

He ascended the throne when but seventeen years of age, extricated his country from many internal and external troubles, organized for it a new system, and became the hero-sovereign of his age. He was one of the greatest of men, in cabinet and in field as well as in faith and humble devotion. He was a broad-minded statesman and patriot, one of the most beloved of rulers, and a philanthropist of the purest order and most comprehensive views. That evangelical Christianity which Luther and his coadjutors exhumed from the superincumbent rubbish of the Middle Ages was dearer to him than his throne or his life. The pure Gospel of Christ was to him the most precious of human possessions. For it he lived, and for it he died. One of his deep-souled hymns, sung along with Luther's **Ein Feste Burg** at the head of his armies in his campaigns for Christian liberty, has its place in our Church-Book to-day. And the bright peculiar star which appeared in the heavens at the time he was born fitly heralded his royal career.

Cut off in the midst of a succession of victories in the thirty-eighth year of his age, the influence of his mind nevertheless served to give another constitution to the Germanic peoples, established the right and power of evangelical Christianity to be and to be unmolested on the earth, and confirmed a new element in the development and progress of the European races and of mankind. With the loftiest conceptions of human life, a thorough acquaintance with the agencies which govern the world, a mind in all respects in thorough subjection to an enlightened Christian conscience, a magnanimity and liberality of sentiment far in advance of his age, and an untarnished devotion which marked his history to its very end, his name stands at the head of the list of illustrious Christian kings and human benefactors.[33]

Note:

[33] Count Galeazzo Gualdo, a Venetian Roman Catholic, who spent some years in both the Imperial and the Swedish armies, says of Gustavus Adolphus that "he was tall, stout, and of such truly royal demeanor that he universally commanded veneration, admiration, love, and fear. His hair and beard were of a light-brown color, his eye large, but not far-sighted. Eloquence dwelt upon his tongue. He spoke German, the native language of his mother, the Swedish, the Latin, the French, and

the Italian languages, and his discourse was agreeable and lively. There never was a general served with so much cheerfulness and devotion as he. He was of an affable and friendly disposition, readily expressing commendation, and noble actions were indelibly fixed upon his memory; on the other hand, excessive politeness and flattery he hated, and if any person approached him in that way he never trusted him."

AXEL OXENSTIERN.

AXEL OXENSTIERN, his friend, companion, and prime minister, was of like mind and character with himself. He was high-born, religiously trained, and thoroughly educated in both theology and law in the best schools which the world then afforded. He was Sweden's greatest and wisest counselor and diplomatist, liberal-minded, true-hearted, dignified, and devout. In religion, in patriotism, in earnest doing for the profoundest interests of man, he was one with his illustrious king. He negotiated the Peace of Kmered with Denmark, the Peace of Stolbowa with Russia, and the armistice with Poland. He accompanied his king in the campaigns in Germany, having charge of all diplomatic affairs and the devising of ways and means for the support of the army in the field, whilst the king commanded it. He won no victories of war, but he was a choice spirit in creating the means by which some of the most valuable of such victories were achieved, and conducted those victories to permanent peace.

When Gustavus Adolphus fell at Luetzen a sacrifice to religious liberty, the whole administration of the kingdom was placed in Oxenstiern's hands. The congress of foreign princes at Heilbronn elected him to the headship of their league against the papal power of Austria; and it was his wisdom and heroism alone which held the league together unto final triumph. Bauer, Torstensson, and Von Wrangle were the flaming swords which finally overwhelmed that power, but the brain which brought the fearful Thirty Years' War to a final close, and established the evangelical cause upon its lasting basis of security by the Peace of Westphalia (1648), was that of Axel Oxenstiern, the very man who sent to Pennsylvania its original colonists as the founders of a free state.

PETER MINUIT.

A kindred spirit was PETER MINUIT, the man whom Oxenstiern selected and commissioned to accompany these first colonists to the west bank of the Delaware, and to act as their president and governor. He too was a high-born, cultured, large-minded Christian man. He was an honored deacon in the Walloon church at Wesel. Removing to Holland, his high qualities led to his selection by the Dutch West India Company as the fittest man to be the first governor and director-general of the Dutch colonies on the Hudson. His great efficiency and public success in that capacity made him the subject of jealousies and accusations, resulting in his recall after five or six years of the most effective administration of the affairs of those colonies. Oxenstiern had the breadth and penetration to understand his real worth, and appointed him the first governor of the New Sweden which since has become the great State of Pennsylvania. He lived less than five years in this new position, and died in Fort Christina, which he built and held during his last years of service on earth. He was a wise, laborious, and far-seeing man, consecrated with all his powers to the formation of a free commonwealth on this then wild territory. His name has largely sunk away from public attention, as the work of the Swedes in general in the founding and fashioning of our commonwealth; but he and they deserve far better than has been awarded them.

A few years ago (1876) some movement was for the first time made to erect a suitable monument to the memory of Minuit. Surely the founder of the greatest city in this Western World, and of the colonial possessions of two European nations, and the first president and governor of the two greatest States in the American Union, ranks among the great historic personages of his period; and his high qualities, noble spirit, and valuable services demand for him a grateful recognition which has been far too slow in coming. There is a debt owing to his name and memory which New York, Pennsylvania, and the American people have not yet duly discharged.

And to these grand men, first of all, are we under obligation of everlasting thanks for our free and happy old commonwealth.

WILLIAM PENN.

But without WILLIAM PENN to reinforce and more fully execute the noble plans, ideas, and beginnings which went before him, things perhaps never would have come to the fortunate results which he was the honored instrument in bringing about.

This man, so renowned in the history of our State, and so specially honored by the peculiar Society of which he was a zealous apostle, was respectably descended. His grandfather was a captain in the English navy, and his father became a distinguished naval officer, who reached high promotion and gave his son the privileges of a good education.

Penn was for three years a student in the University of Oxford, until expelled, with others, for certain offensive non-conformities. He was not what we would call religiously trained, but he was endowed with a strong religious nature, even bordering on fanaticism, so that he needed only the application of the match to set his whole being aglow and active with the profoundest zeal, whether wise or otherwise. And that match was early applied.

When England had reached the summit of delirium under her usurping Protector, Oliver Cromwell, there arose, among many other sects full of enthusiastic self-assertion, that of the Quakers, who were chiefly characterized by a profound religious, and oft fanatical, opposition to the Established Church, as well as to the Crown. Coming in contact with one of their most zealous preachers, young Penn was inflamed with their spirit and became a vigorous propagator of their particular style of devotion.

As the Quaker tenets respected the state as well as religion, the bold avowal of them brought him into collision with the laws, and several times into prison and banishment. But, so far from intimidating him, this only the more confirmed him in his convictions and fervency. By his familiarity with able theologians, such as Dr. Owen and Bishop Tillotson, as well as from his own studies of the Scriptures, he was deeply grounded in the main principles of the evangelic faith. Indeed, he was in many things, in his later life, much less a Quaker than many who glory in his name, and all his sons after him found their religious home in the Church of England, which, to Quakers generally, was a very Babylon. But he was an honest-minded, pure, and cultured Christian believer, holding firmly to the inward elements of the orthodox faith in God and Christ, in revelation and eternal judgment, in the rights of man and the claims of justice. If some of his friends and representatives did not deal as honorably with the Swedes in respect to their prior titles to their improved lands as right and charity would require, it is not to be set down to his personal reproach. And his zeal for his sect and his genuine devotion to God and religious liberty, together with a large-hearted philanthropy, were the springs which moved him to seize the opportunity which offered in the settlement of his deceased father's claim on the government to secure a grant of territory and privilege to form a free state in America--first for his own, and then for all other persecuted people.

AN ESTIMATE OF PENN.

It may be that Penn has been betimes a little overrated. He has, and deserves, a high place in the history of our commonwealth, but he was not the real founder of it; for its foundations were laid years before he was born and more than forty years before he received his charter. He founded Pennsylvania only as Americus Vespucius discovered America. Neither was he the author of those elements of free government, equal rights, and religious liberty which have characterized our commonwealth. They were the common principles of Luther and the Reformation, and were already largely embodied for this very territory[34] long before Penn's endeavors, as also, in measure, in the Roman Catholic colony of Maryland from the same source.

Nor was he, in his own strength, possessed of so much wise forethought and profound legislative and executive ability as that with which he is sometimes credited. But he was a conscientious, earnest, and God-fearing man, cultured by education and grace, gifted with admirable address, sincere and philanthropic in his aims, and guided and impelled by circumstances and a peculiar religious zeal which Providence overruled to ends far greater than his own intentions or thoughts.

Note:

[34] See sketch of the plan of Gustavus Adolphus for his colony, page 143, and the instructions given to Governor Printz in 1642.

PENN AND THE INDIANS.

What is called Penn's particular policy toward the Indians, and the means of his successes in that regard, existed in practical force scores of years before he arrived. His celebrated treaties with them, as far as they were fact, were but continuations and repetitions between them and the English, which had long before been made between them and the Swedes, who did more for these barbarian peoples than he, and who helped him in the matter more than he helped himself.

We are not fully informed respecting all the first instructions given to Governor Minuit when he came hither with Pennsylvania's original colony in 1637-38, but there is every reason to infer that they strictly corresponded to those given to his successor, Governor Printz, five years afterward, on his appointment in 1642, about which there can be no question. Minuit entered into negotiations with the

Indians the very first thing on his landing, and purchased from them, as the rightful proprietors, all the land on the western side of the river from Henlopen to Trenton Falls; a deed for which was regularly drawn up, to which the Indians subscribed their hands and marks. Posts were also driven into the ground as landmarks of this treaty, which were still visible in their places sixty years afterward.

In the appointment and commission of Governor Printz it was commanded him to "bear in mind the articles of contract entered into with the wild inhabitants of the country as its rightful lords." "The wild nations bordering on all other sides the governor shall understand how to treat with all humanity and respect, that no violence, or wrong be done them; but he shall rather at every opportunity exert himself that the same wild people may gradually be instructed in the truths and worship of the Christian religion, and in other ways brought to civilization and good government, and in this manner properly guided. Especially shall he seek to gain their confidence, and impress upon their minds that neither he, the governor, nor his people and subordinates, are come into those parts to do them any wrong or injury."

This policy was not a thing of mere coincidence. It was the express stipulation and command of the throne of Sweden, August 15, 1642, which was two years before William Penn was born; and "this policy was steadily pursued and adhered to by the Swedes during the whole time of their continuance in America, as the governors of the territory of which they had thus acquired the possession; and the consequences were of the most satisfactory character. They lived in peace with the Indians, and received no injuries from them. The Indians respected them, and long after the Swedish power had disappeared from the shores of the Delaware they continued to cherish its memory and speak of it with confidence and affection."[35]

Governor Printz arrived in this country in 1642, and with him came Rev. John Campanius as chaplain and pastor of the Swedish colony. His grandson, Thomas Campanius Holm, many years after published numerous items put on record by the elder Campanius, in which it appears that the commands to Printz respecting the Indians were very scrupulously carried out.

According to these records, the Indians were very familiar at the house of the elder Campanius, and he did much to teach and Christianize them. "He generally succeeded in making them understand that there is one Lord God, self-existent and one in three Persons; how the same God made the world, and made man, from whom all other men have descended; how Adam afterward disobeyed, sinned against his Creator, and involved all his descendants in condemnation; how God sent his only-begotten Son Jesus Christ into the world, who was born of the Virgin Mary and suffered for the saving of men; how he died upon the cross, and was raised again the third day; and, lastly, how, after forty days, he ascended into heaven, whence he will return at a future day to judge the living and the dead," etc. And so much interest did they take in these instructions, and seemed so well disposed to embrace Christianity, that Campanius was induced to study and master their language, that he might the more effectually teach them the religion of Christ. He also translated into the Indian language the Catechism of Luther, perhaps the very first book ever put into the Indian tongue.

Campanius began his work of evangelizing these wild people four years before Eliot, who is sometimes called "the morning star of missionary enterprise," but who first commenced his labors in New England only in 1646. Hence Dr. Clay remarks that "the Swedes may claim the honor of having been the first missionaries among the Indians, at least in Pennsylvania."[36] "It was, *in fact, the Swedes who inaugurated the peaceful policy of William Penn*. This was not an accidental circumstance in the Swedish policy, but was deliberately adopted and always carefully observed."[37]

When Mr. Rising became governor of the Swedish colony he invited ten Indian chiefs, or kings, to a friendly conference with him. It was held at Tinicum, on the Delaware, June 17, 1654, when the governor saluted them, in the name of the Swedish queen, with assurances of every kindness toward them, and proposed to them a firm renewal of the old friendship. Campanius has given a minute account of this conference, and recites the speech in which one of the chiefs, named Naaman, testified how good the Swedes had been to them; that the Swedes and Indians had been in the time of Governor Printz as one body and one heart; that they would henceforward be as one head, like the calabash, which has neither rent nor seam, but one piece without a crack; and that in case of danger to the Swedes they would ever serve and defend them. It was at the same time further arranged and agreed that if any trespasses were committed by any of their people upon the property of the Swedes, the matter should be investigated by men chosen from both sides, and the person found guilty "should be punished for it as a warning to others."[38] This occurred when William Penn was but ten years of age, and twenty-eight years before his arrival in America.

And upon the subject of the help which the Swedes rendered to Penn in his dealings with these people in the long after years, Acrelius writes: "The Proprietor ingratiated himself with the Indians. The Swedes acted as his interpreters, especially Captain Lars (Lawrence) Kock, who was a great favorite among the Indians. He was sent to New York to buy goods suitable for traffic. He did all he could to give them a good opinion of their new ruler" (p. 114); and it was by means of the aid and endeavors of the Swedes, more than by any influence of his own, that Penn came to the standing with these people to which he attained, and on which his fame in that regard rests.

Note:

[35] Introduction to Acrelius's ***History***.

[36] ***Swedish Annals***, p. 26.

[37] Dr. Reynolds's ***Introduction to Acrelius***, p. 14.

[38] See Acrelius's ***History***, pp. 64, 65, and Clay's ***Swedish Annals***, pp. 24, 25. PENN'S WORK.

But still, as a man, a colonist, a governor, and a friend of the race, we owe to William Penn great honor and respect, and his arrival here is amply worthy of our grateful commemoration. The location and framing of this goodly city, and a united and consolidated Pennsylvania established finally in its original principles of common rights and common freedom, are his lasting monument. If he was not the spring of our colonial existence, he was its reinforcement by a strong and fortunate stream, which more fully determined the channel of its history. If the doctrine of liberty of conscience and religion, the principles of toleration and common rights, and the embodying of them in a free state open to all sufferers for conscience' sake, did not originate with him, he performed a noble work and contributed a powerful influence toward their final triumph and permanent establishment on this territory. And his career, taken all in all, connects his name with an illustrious service to the cause of freedom, humanity, and even Christianity, especially in its more practical and ethical bearings.

THE GREATNESS OF FAITH.

Such, then, were the men most concerned in founding and framing our grand old commonwealth. They were men of faith, men of thorough culture, men of mark by birth and station, men who had learned to grapple with the great problem of human rights, human happiness, human needs, and human relations to heaven and earth. They believed in God, in the revelation of God, in the Gospel of Christ, in the responsibility of the soul to its Maker, and in the demands of a living charity toward God and all his creatures. And their religious faith and convictions constituted the fire which set them in motion and sustained and directed their exertions for the noble ends which it is ours so richly to enjoy. Had they not been the earnest Christians that they were, they never could have been the men they proved themselves, nor ever have thought the thoughts or achieved the glorious works for ever connected with their names.

We are apt to contemplate Christian faith and devotion only in its more private and personal effects on individual souls, the light and peace it brings to the true believer, and the purification and hope it works in the hearts of those who receive it, whilst we overlook its force upon the great world outside and its shapings of the facts and currents of history. We think of Luther wrestling with his sins, despairing and dying under the impossible task of working out for himself an availing righteousness, and rejoice with him in the light and peace which came to his agonized soul through the grand and all-conditioning doctrine of justification by simple faith in an all-sufficient Redeemer; but we do not always realize how the breaking of that evangelic principle into his earnest heart was the incarnation of a power which divided the Christian ages, brought the world over the summit of the water-shed, and turned the gravitation of the laboring nations toward a new era of liberty and happiness. And so we refer to the spiritual training of a Gustavus Adolphus and an Axel Oxenstiern in the simple truths of Luther's Catechism and the restored Gospel, and to the opening of the heart of a William Penn to the exhortations of Friend Loe to forsake the follies of the corrupt world and seek his portion with the pure in heaven, and mark the unfoldings of their better nature which those blessed instructions wrought; whilst we fail to note that therein lay the springs and germs which have given us our grand commonwealth and established for us the free institutions of Church and State in which we so much glory and rejoice.

Ah, yes; there is greatness and good and blessing untold for man and for the world in the personal hearing, believing, and heeding of the Word and testimony of God. No man can tell to what new impulses in human history, or to what new currents of benediction and continents of national glory, it may lead for souls in the school of Christ to open themselves meekly to the inflowings of Heaven's free grace. It was the sowing of God's truth and the planting of God's Spirit in these men's hearts that most of all grew for us our country and our blessed liberties.

II. THE PRINCIPLES ENTHRONED.

The religious element in man is the deepest and most powerful in his nature. It is that also which asserts and claims the greatest independence from external constraints. It is therefore the height of unwisdom, not to say tyranny, for earthly magistracy to interfere by penalty and sword with the religious opinions and movements of the people, so long as civil authority and public order are not invaded and the rights of others are not infringed. In such cases it is always best to combat only with the Word of God. If of men it will come to naught, and if of God it cannot be suppressed. Reaction against wrongs done to truth and right is sure to come, and will push through to revolution and victory in spite of all unrighteous power. It is vain for any human governments to think to chain up the honest convictions of the soul. God made it free, and sooner or later it will be free, in spite of everything.

It was largely the weight and current of such reaction against arbitrary interference with the religious convictions and free conscience of man that furnished the impulse to the original peopling of our State and country, and gave shape to the constitution and laws of this commonwealth for the last two hundred years. Nor will our inquiries and showings with regard to the founding of Pennsylvania be complete without something more respecting the leading principles which governed in that fortunate movement.

OUR STATE THE PRODUCT OF FAITH.

I. It is a matter of indisputable fact that the founding of our commonwealth was one of the direct fruits of the revived Gospel of Christ. But a little searching into the influences most active in the history is required to show that it was religious conviction and faith, more than anything else, that had to do with the case.

Changes had come. Luther had found the Bible chained, and set it free. Apostolic Christianity had reappeared, and was re-uttering itself with great power among the nations. Its quickening truths and growing victories were undermining the gigantic usurpations and falsehoods which for ages had been oppressing our world. Conscience, illuminated and revived by the Word of God, had risen up to assert its rights of free judgment and free worship, and resentful power had drawn the sword to put it down. Continental Europe was being deluged with blood and devastated by relentless religious wars to crush out the evangelic faith, whose confessors held up the Bible over all popes and secular powers, and would not consent to part with their inalienable charter from the throne of Heaven to worship God according to his Word. And amid these woeful struggles the good providence of the Almighty opened up to the attention of the nations the vast new territories of this Western World.

From various motives, indeed, were the several original colonies of America founded. Some of the colonists came from a spirit of adventure. Some came for territorial aggrandizement and national enrichment. Some came as mercantile speculators. And each of these considerations may have entered somewhat into the most of these colonization schemes. But it was mainly flight from oppression on account of religious convictions which influenced the first colony of New England, and a still freer religious motive induced the colonization of Pennsylvania.

All the men most concerned in the matter were profoundly religious men and thorough and active believers in revived Christianity; and it was most of all from these religious feelings and impulses that they acted in the case.

GUSTAVUS AND THE SWEDES.

The first presentation to the king of Sweden, by William Usselinx, touching the planting of a colony on the west bank of the Delaware, looked to the establishment of a trading company with unlimited trading privileges; and the argument for it was the great source of revenue it would be to the kingdom. But when Gustavus Adolphus entered into the subject and gave his royal favor to it, quite other motives and considerations came in to determine his course. As the history records, and quite aside from the prospect of establishing his power in these parts of the world, "the king, whose zeal for the honor of God was not less ardent than for the welfare of his subjects, *availed himself of this opportunity to extend the doctrines of Christ among the heathen*,"[39] and to this end granted letters patent, in which it was further provided that a free state should be formed, guaranteeing all personal rights of property, honor, and religion, and forming an asylum and place of security for the persecuted people of all nations. And when these gracious intentions of the king were revived after his death, the same ideas and provisions were carefully maintained, specially stipulating (1) for every human respect toward the Indians--to wit, that the governors of the colony should deal justly with them as the rightful lords of the land, and exert themselves at every opportunity "that the same wild people may be instructed in the truths and worship of the Christian religion, and in other ways brought to civilization and good government, and in this manner properly guided;" (2) "above all things to consider and see to it that divine service be duly maintained and zealously performed according to the unaltered Augsburg Confession;" and (3) to protect those of a different confession in the free exercise of their own forms.[40]

It is plain, therefore, that the spirit of religion, the spirit of evangelical missions, the spirit of Christian charity, and the spirit of devotion to the protection of religious liberty and freedom of conscience were the dominating motives on the part of those who founded the first permanent settlement on the territory of Pennsylvania.

Note:

[39] *History of New Sweden*, by Israel Acrelius, p. 21.

[40] Rehearsed in the commission to Governor Printz, 1642, sections 9 and 26.

THE FEELINGS OF WILLIAM PENN.

Bating somewhat the missionary character of the enterprise, the same may be said of William Penn and his great reinforcement to what had thus been successfully begun long before his time. He was himself a very zealous preacher of religion, though more in the line of protest against the world and the existing Church than in the line of positive Christianity and the conversion and evangelization of the heathen. He had himself been a great sufferer for his religious convictions, along with the people whose cause he had espoused and made his own. His controlling desire was to honor and glorify God in the founding of a commonwealth in which those of his way of thinking might have a secure home of their own and worship their Creator as best agreed with their feelings and convictions, without being molested or disturbed; offering at the same time the same precious boon to others in like constraints willing to share the lot of his endeavors.

The motives of Charles II. in granting his charter were, first of all, to discharge a heavy pecuniary claim of Penn against the government on account of his father; next, to honor the memory and merits of the late Admiral Penn; and, finally, at the same time, to "favor William Penn in his laudable efforts to enlarge the British empire, to promote the trade and prosperity of the kingdom, and to reduce the savage nations by just and gentle measures to the love of civilized life and the Christian religion." Penn's idea, as stated by his memorialist, was "to obtain the grant of a territory on the west side of the Delaware, in which he might not only furnish an asylum to Friends (Quakers), and others who were persecuted on account of their religious persuasion, but might erect a government upon principles approaching much nearer the standard of evangelical purity than any which had been previously raised."

His own account of the matter is: "For my country I eyed the Lord in obtaining it; and more was I drawn inward to look to him, and to owe it to his hand and power, than to any other way. I have so obtained it, and desire to keep it, that I may not be unworthy of his love, but do that which may answer his kind providence and serve his truth and people, that an example may be set up to the nations. There may be room there, though not here, for such an holy experiment." "I do therefore desire the Lord's wisdom to guide me and those that may be concerned with me, that we may do the thing that is truly wise and just."

And with these aims and this spirit he invited people to join him, came to the territory which had been granted him, conferred with the Swedish and Dutch colonists already on the ground, and together with them established the Commonwealth of Pennsylvania.

RECOGNITION OF THE DIVINE BEING.

II. Accordingly, also, the chief corner-stone in the constitutional fabric of our State was the united official acknowledgment of the being and supremacy of one eternal and ever-living God, the Judge of all men and the Lord of nations.

The self-existence and government of Almighty God is the foundation of all things. Nothing *is* without him. And the devout and dutiful recognition of him and the absolute supremacy of his laws are the basis and chief element of everything good and stable in human affairs. He who denies this or fails in its acknowledgment is so far practically self-stultified, beside himself, outside the sphere of sound rationality, and incapable of rightly understanding or directing himself or anything else. Nor could those who founded our commonwealth have been moved as they were, or achieved the happy success they did, had it not been for their clear, profound, and practical acknowledgment of the being and government of that good and almighty One who fills immensity and eternity, and from whom, and by whom, and to whom are all things.

Some feel and act as if it were an imbecility, or a thing only for the weak, timid, and helpless, to be concerned about an Almighty God. But greater, braver, and more manly men did not then exist than those who were most prominent and active in founding and framing our commonwealth; and of all men then making themselves felt in the affairs of our world, they were among the most honest and devout in the practical confession of the eternal being and providence of Jehovah.

The great Gustavus Adolphus and the equally great Axel Oxenstiern held and confessed from their deepest souls and in all their thoughts and doings that there is an eternal God, infinite in power, wisdom, and goodness, the Creator, Preserver, and Judge of all things, visible and invisible, and that on him and his favor alone all good and prosperity in this world and the next depends. This they ever formally and devoutly set forth in all their state papers and in all their undertakings and doings, whether as men or as rulers. The sound of songs and prayers to this almighty and ever-present God was heard at every sunrise through all the army of Gustavus in the field, as well as in the tent and closet of its great commander. And all the instructions given to the governors of the colony on the Delaware were meekly conditioned to the will of God, with specific emphasis on the provision: "Above all things, shall the governor consider and see to it that a true and due worship, becoming honor, laud, and praise be paid to the Most High in all things."

The same is true of William Penn. From early life he was always a zealous exhorter to the devout worship of Almighty God as the only Illuminator and Helper of men. What he averred in his letter to the Indians was the great root-principle of his life: "There is a great God and Power, which hath made the world and all things therein, to whom you and I and all people owe their being and well-being, and to whom you and I must one day give an account for all that we have done in this world."

And what was thus wrought into the texture of his being he also wove into the original constitution of our State.

ENACTMENTS ON THE SUBJECT.

All the articles of government and regulation ordained by the first General Assembly, held at Upland (Chester) from the seventh to the tenth day of December, 1682, were fundamentally grounded on this express "Whereas, the glory of Almighty God and the good of mankind is the reason and end of government, and therefore government itself is a valuable ordinance of God; and forasmuch as it is principally desired to make and establish such laws as shall best preserve true Christian and civil liberty, in opposition to all unchristian, licentious, and unjust practices, whereby God may have his due, Caesar his due, and the people their due, from tyranny and oppression on the one side, and insolence and licentiousness on the other; so that the best and firmest foundation may be laid for the present and future happiness of both the governor and the people of this province and their posterity;" for it was deemed and believed on all hands that neither permanence nor happiness, enduring order nor prosperity, could come from any other principle than that of the recognition of the supremacy and laws of Him from whom all things proceed and on whom all creatures depend.

On this wise also ran the very first of the sixty-one laws ordained by that Assembly: "Almighty God being the Lord of conscience, Father of lights, and the Author as well as Object of all divine knowledge, faith, and worship, who alone can enlighten the mind and convince the understanding of people in due reverence to his sovereignty over the souls of mankind," the rights of citizenship, protection, and liberty should be to every person, then or thereafter residing in this province, "who shall confess one Almighty God to be the Creator, Upholder, and Ruler of the world, and profess himself obliged in conscience to live peaceably and justly under the civil government;" provided, further, that no person antagonizing this confession, or refusing to profess the same, or convicted of unsober or dishonest conversation, should ever hold office in this commonwealth.

And so entirely did this, and what else was then and there enacted and ordained, fall in with the teachings, feelings, and beliefs of the hardy and devoted Swedish Lutherans, who had here been professing and fulfilling the same for two scores of years preceding, that they not only joined in the making of these enactments, but sent a special deputation to the governor formally to assure him that, on these principles and the faithful administration of them, they would love, serve, and obey him with all they possessed.

IMPORTANCE OF THIS PRINCIPLE.

Nor can it ever be known in this world how much of the success, prosperity, and happy conservatism which have marked this commonwealth in all the days and years since, have come directly from this planting of it on the grand corner-stone of all national stability, order, and happiness. Surely, a widely different course and condition of things would have come but for this secure anchoring of the ship on the everlasting Rock. And a thousand pities it is that the influence of French atheism was allowed to exclude so wholesome a principle from the Declaration of our national Independence and from our national Constitution. Whilst such recognition of Jehovah's supremacy and government abides in living force in the hearts of the people, the absence of its official formulation may be of no material disadvantage; but for the better preservation of it in men's minds, and for the obstruction of the insidious growth of what strikes at the foundation of all government and order, it would have been well had the same been put in place as the grand corner-stone of our whole national fabric, as it was in the original organization of the Commonwealth of Pennsylvania, and kept in both clear and unchangeable for ever. We might then hope for better things than are indicated by the present drift, and the outlook for those to come after us would be less dark and doubtful than it is.

But, since weakenings and degeneration in these respects have come into the enactments of public power, it is all the more needful for every true and patriotic citizen to be earnest and firm in witnessing for God and his everlasting laws, that the people may be better than the later expressions of their state documents. The example of the fathers makes appeal to the consciences of their children not to let go from our hearts and lives the deep and abiding recognition and confession of that almighty Governor of all things from whose righteous tribunal no one living can escape, and before whom no contemner of his authority can stand.

RELIGIOUS LIBERTY.

III. Another great and precious principle enthroned in the founding of our commonwealth was that of religious liberty.

One of the saddest chapters in human history is that of persecution on account of religious convictions--the imposition of penalties, torture, and death by the sword of government on worthy people because of their honest opinions of duty to Almighty God. For the punishment of the lawless, the wicked, and the intractable, and for the praise, peace, and protection of them that do well, the civil magistrate is truly the authorized representative of God, and fails in his office and duty where the powers he wields are not studiously and vigorously exercised to these ends. But God hath reserved to himself, and hath not committed to any creature hands, the power and dominion to interfere with realm of conscience. As he alone can instruct and govern it, and as its sphere is that of the recognition of his will and law and the soul's direct amenability to his judgment-bar, it is a gross usurpation and a wicked presumption for any other authority or power to undertake to force obedience contrary to the soul's persuasion of what its Maker demands of it as a condition of his favor.

It is a principle of human action and obligation recognized in both Testaments, that when the requirements of human authority conflict with those of the Father of spirits we must obey God rather than man. The rights of conscience and the rights of God thus coincide, and to trample on the one is to deny the other. And when earthly governments invade this sacred territory they invade the exclusive domain of God and make war upon the very authority from which they have their right to be.

The plea of its necessity for the support of orthodoxy, the maintenance of the truth, and the glory of God will not avail for its justification, for God has not ordained civil government to inflict imprisonment, exile, and death upon religious dissenters, or even heretics; and his truth and glory he has arranged to take care of in quite another fashion. What Justin Martyr and Tertullian in the early Church and Luther in the Reformation-time declared, must for ever stand among the settled verities of Heaven: that it is not right to murder, burn, and afflict people because they feel in conscience bound to a belief and course of life which they have found and embraced as the certain will and requirement of their Maker. We must ward off heresy with the sword of the Spirit, which is the Word of God, and not with the sword of the state and with fire.

PERSECUTION FOR OPINION'S SAKE.

And yet such abuses of power have been staining and darkening all the ages of human administration, and, unfortunately, among professing Christians as well as among pagans and Jews. Intolerance is so rooted in the selfishness and ambition of human nature that it has ever been one of the most difficult of practical problems to curb and regulate it. Those who have most complained of it whilst feeling it, often only needed to have the circumstances reversed in order to fall into similar wickedness. The Puritans, who fled from it as from the Dragon himself, soon had their Star-Chamber too, their whipping-posts, their death-scaffolds, and their sentences of exile for those who dissented from their orthodoxy and their order. Even infidelity and atheism, always the most blatant for freedom when in the minority, have shown in the philosophy of Hobbes and in the Reign of Terror in France that they are as liable to be intolerant, fanatical, and oppressive when they have the mastery as the strongest faith and the most assured religionism. And the Quakers themselves, who make freedom of conscience one of the chief corner-stones of their religion, have not always been free from offensive and disorderly aggressions upon the rightful sphere of government and the rightful religious freedom of other worshipers. Even so treacherous is the human heart on the subject of just and equal religious toleration.

SPIRIT OF THE FOUNDERS.

It is therefore a matter of everlasting gratitude and thanksgiving that all the men most concerned in the founding of our commonwealth were so clear and well-balanced on the subject of religious liberty, and so thoroughly inwove the same into its organic constitution.

Gustavus Adolphus and Axel Oxenstiern were the heroes of their time in the cause of religious liberty in continental Europe. Though intensely troubled in their administration by the Roman Catholics and the Anabaptists, the most intolerant of intolerants in those days, they never opposed force against the beliefs or worships of either; and when force was used against the papal powers, it was only so far as to preserve unto themselves and their fellow-confessors the inalienable right to worship God according to the dictates of their own consciences without molestation or disturbance. In their scheme of colonization in this Western World, first and last, the invitation was to all classes of Christians in suffering and persecution for conscience' sake, who were favorable to a free state where they could have the free enjoyment of their property and religion, to cast in their lot. In the first charter, confirmed by all the authorities of the kingdom and rehearsed in the instructions given by the throne for the execution of the intention, special provision was made for the protection of the convictions and worship of those not of the same confession with that for which the government provided. Though a Lutheran colony, under a Lutheran king, sustained and protected by a Lutheran government, the Calvinists had place and equal protection in it from the very beginning; and when the Quakers came, they were at once and as freely welcomed on the same free principles, as also the representatives of the Church of England.

As to William Penn, though contemplating above all the well-being and furtherance of the particular Society of which he was an eminent ornament and preacher, consistency with himself, as well as the established situation of affairs, demanded of him the free toleration of the Church, however unpalatable to his Society, and with it of all religious sects and orders of worship. From his prison at Newgate he had written that the enaction of laws restraining persons from the free exercise of their consciences in matters of religion was but "the knotting of whip-cord on the part of the enactors to lash their own posterity, whom they could never promise to be conformed for ages to come to a national religion." Again and again had he preached and proclaimed the folly and wickedness of attempting to change the religious opinions of men by the application of force--the utter unreasonableness of persecuting orderly people in this world about things which belong to the next--the gross injustice of sacrificing any one's liberty or property on account of creed if not found breaking the laws relating to natural and civil things.

Hence, from principle as well as from necessity, when he came to formulate a political constitution for his colony, he laid it down as the primordial principle: "I do, for me and mine, declare and establish for the first fundamental of the government of my province that every person that doth and shall reside therein shall have and enjoy the free possession of his or her faith and exercise of worship toward God, in such way and manner as every such person shall in conscience believe is most acceptable to God. And so long as such person useth not this Christian liberty to licentiousness or the destruction of others--that is, to speak loosely and profanely or contemptuously of God, Christ, the Holy Scriptures, or religion, or commit any moral evil or injury against others in their conversation--he or she shall be protected in the enjoyment of the aforesaid Christian liberty by the civil magistrate."

CONSTITUTIONAL PROVISIONS.

This was in exact accord with the principles and provisions under which the original colony had been formed, and had already been living and prospering for more than forty years preceding. Everything, therefore, was in full readiness and condition for the universal and hearty adoption of the grand first article enacted by the first General Assembly, to wit: "That no person now or hereafter residing in this province, who shall confess one Almighty God to be the Creator, Upholder, and Ruler of the world, and profess himself obliged in conscience to live peaceably and justly under the civil government, shall in any wise be molested or prejudiced on account of his conscientious persuasion or practice; nor shall he be compelled to frequent or maintain any religious worship, place, or ministry contrary to his mind, but shall freely enjoy his liberty in that respect, without interruption or reflection."

In these specific provisions all classes in the colony at the time heartily united. And thus was secured and guaranteed to every good citizen that full, rightful, and precious religious freedom which is the birthright of all Americans, for which the oppressed of all the ages sighed, and which had to make its way through a Red Sea of human tears and blood and many a sorrowful wilderness before reaching its place of rest.

SAFEGUARDS TO TRUE LIBERTY.

IV. But the religious liberty which our fathers thus sought to secure and to transmit to their posterity was not a licentious libertinism. They knew the value of religious principles and good morals to the individual and to the state, and they did not leave it an open matter, under plea of free conscience, for men to conduct themselves as they please with regard to virtue and religion.

To be disrespectful toward divine worship, to interfere with its free exercise as honest men are moved to render it, or to set at naught the moral code of honorable behavior in human society, is never the dictate of honest conviction of duty, and, in the nature of things, cannot be. It is not conscience, but the overriding of conscience; nay, rebellion against the whole code of conscience, against the foundations of all government, against the very existence of civil society. Liberty to blaspheme Almighty God, to profane his name and ordinances, to destroy his worship, and to set common morality at naught, is not religious liberty, but disorderly wickedness, a cloak of maliciousness, the licensing of the devil as an angel of light. It belongs to mere brute liberty, which must be restrained and brought under bonds in order to render true liberty possible. Wild and lawless freedom must come under the restraints and limits of defined order, peace, and essential morality, or somebody's freedom must suffer, and social happiness is out of the question. And it is one of the inherent aims and offices of government to enforce this very constraint, without which it totally fails of its end and forfeits its right to be. Where people are otherwise law-abiding, orderly, submissive to the requisites for the being and well-being of a state, and abstain from encroachments upon the liberties of others, they are not to be molested, forced, or compelled in spiritual matters contrary to their honest convictions; but public blasphemy, open profanity, disorderly interference with divine worship and reverence, and the hindrance of what tends to the preservation of good morals, it pertains to the existence and office of a state to restrain and punish. Severity upon such disorders is not tyrannical abridgment of the rights of conscience, for no proper citizen's conscience can ever prompt or constrain him to any such things. And everything which tends to weaken and destroy regard for the eternal Power on which all things depend, to relax the sense of accountability to the divine judgment, and to trample on the laws of eternal morality, is the worst enemy of the state, which it cannot allow without peril to its own existence.

On the other hand, the state is bound for the same reasons to protect and defend religion in general and the cultivation of the religious sentiments, in so far, at least, as the laws of virtue and order are not transgressed in the name of religion. It may not interfere to decide between different religious societies or churches, as they may be equally conscientious and honest in their diversities; but where the tendency is to good and reverence, and the training of the community to right and orderly life, it belongs to the office and being of the state not only to tolerate, but to protect them all alike. In the fatherly care of its subjects, the people consenting, the state may also recommend and provide support for some particular and approved order of faith and worship, just as it provides for public education. And though the civil power may not rightfully punish, fine, imprison, and oppress orderly and honest citizens for conscientious non-conformity to any one specific system of belief and worship, it may, and must, provide for and protect what tends to its rightful conservation, and also condemn, punish, and restrain whatsoever tends to unseat it and undermine its existence and peace. These are fundamental requirements in all sound political economy.

LAWS ON RELIGION AND MORALS.

Our fathers, in their wisdom, understood this, and fashioned their state provisions and laws accordingly.

The thing specified as the supreme concern of the public authorities in the original settlement of this territory by the Swedes was, to "consider and see to it that a true and due worship, becoming honor, laud, and praise be paid to the most high God in all things," and that "all persons, but especially the young, shall be duly instructed in the articles of their Christian faith."

But if public worship and religious instruction are to be fostered and preserved by the state, there must be set times for it, the people released at those times from hindering occupations and engagements, and whatever may interfere therewith restrained and put under bonds against interruption. In other words, the Lord's proper worship demands and requires a protected Lord's Day. Such appointed and sacred times for these holy purposes have been from the foundation of the world. Under all dispensations one day in every seven was a day unto the Lord, protected and preserved for such sacred uses, on which secular occupations should cease, and nothing allowed which would interfere with the public worship of Almighty God and the handling of his Word. And "because it was requisite to appoint a certain day, that the people might know when they ought to come together, it appears that the Christian Church [and so all Christian states] did for that purpose appoint the Lord's Day," our weekly Sunday.

This William Penn found in existence and observance by the Swedes and the Dutch on this territory when he arrived. He therefore advised, and the first General Assembly of Pennsylvania justly ordained, "that, according to the good example of the primitive Christians and the ease of the creation, every first day of the week, called the Lord's Day, people shall abstain from their common daily labor, that they may the better dispose themselves to worship God according to their understandings"--a provision so necessary and important that the statute laws of our commonwealth have always guarded its observance with penalties which the State cannot in justice to itself allow to go unenforced, and which no good citizen should refuse strictly to obey.

And to the same end was it provided and ordained by the first General Assembly that "if any person shall abuse or deride another for his different persuasion or practice in religion, such shall be looked upon as disturbers of the peace, and be punished accordingly." And in the line of the same wholesome and necessary policy it was also further provided and ordained that "all such offences against God as swearing, cursing, lying, profane talking, drunkenness, obscene words, revels, etc. etc., which excite the people to rudeness, cruelty, and irreligion, shall be respectively discouraged and severely punished."

Such were the good and righteous provisions made for the restraint of the licentiousness and brutishness of man in the primeval days of our commonwealth; and wherein it has since sunk away from these original organic laws the people have only weakened and degraded themselves, and hindered that virtuous and happy prosperity which would otherwise in far larger degree than now be our inheritance.

FORMS OF GOVERNMENT.

V. And yet again, as the fathers of our commonwealth gave us religion without compulsion, so they also gave us a State without a king.

There is nothing necessarily wrong or necessarily right in this particular. Monarchy, aristocracy, republicanism, or pure democracy cannot claim divine right the one over against the other. Either may be good, or either may be bad, as the situation and the chances may be. There has been as much bloody wrong and ruin wrought in the name of liberty as in the establishment of thrones. There have been as good and happy governments by kings as by any other methods of human administration. Civil authority is essential to man, and the power for it must lie somewhere. The only question is as to the safest depository of it. The mere form of the government is no great matter. It has been justly said, "There is hardly a government in the world so ill designed that in good hands would not do well enough, nor any so good that in ill hands can do aught great and good." Governments depend on men, not men on governments. Let men be good, and the government will not be bad; but if men are bad, no government will hold for good. If government be bad, good men will cure it; and if the government be good, bad men will warp and spoil it. Nor is there any form of government known to man that is not liable to abuse, prostitution, tyranny, unrighteousness, and oppression.

The best government is that which most efficiently conserves the true ends of government, be the form what it may. Anything differing from this is worthless sentimentalism, undeserving of sober regard. And to meet the true ends of government there must be power to enforce obedience, and there must be checks upon that power to secure its subjects against its abuse; for "liberty without obedience is confusion, and obedience without liberty is slavery." But there may be liberty under monarchy, as well as reverence and obedience under democracy, whilst there may be oppression and bloody tyranny under either.

Amid the varied experiments of the ages the human mind is more and more settling itself in favor of mixed forms of government, in which the rights of the people and the limitations of authority are set down in fixed constitutions, taking the direct rule from the multitude, but still holding the rulers accountable to the people. Such were more or less the forms under which the founders of our commonwealth were tutored.

A REPUBLICAN STATE.

But they went a degree further than the precedents before them. They believed the safest depository of power to be with the people themselves, under constitutions ordained by those intending to live under them and administered by persons of their own choice. "Where the laws rule, and the people are a party to those laws," was believed to be the true ideal and realization of civil liberty--the way "to support power in reverence with the people, and to secure the people from the abuse of power, that they may be free by their just obedience, and the magistrates honorable for their just administration."

And with these ideas, "with reverence to God and good conscience to men," the first General Assembly in 1682 enacted a common code of sixty-one laws, in which the foundation-stones of the civil and criminal jurisprudence of this broad commonwealth were laid, and a style of government ordained so reasonable, moderate, just, and equal in its provisions that no one yet has found just cause to deny the wisdom and beneficence of its structure, whilst Montesquieu pronounces it "an instance unparalleled in the world's history of the foundation of a great state laid in peace, justice, and equality."

THE LAST TWO HUNDRED YEARS.

Two hundred years have gone by since this completed organization of our noble commonwealth. Her free and liberal principles then still remained in large measure to be learned by some of the other American colonies. From the very start she was the chief conservator of what was to be the model for all this grand Union of free States--a character which she has never lost in all the history of our national existence. Six generations of stalwart freemen has she reared beneath her shielding care to people her own vast territory and that of many other States, no one of which has ever failed in truthfulness to the great principles in which she was born. Always more solid than noisy, and more reserved than obtrusive, she has ever served as the great balance-wheel in the mighty engine of our national organization. Her life, commingled with other lives attempered to her own, now pulsates from ocean to ocean and from the frozen lakes to the warm Gulf waters, all glad and glorious in the unity and sunshine of constitutional government in the hands of a free people. With her population drawn from all nationalities to learn from her lips the sacred lessons of independent self-rule, she has sent it forth as freely to the westward to build co-equal States in the beauty of her own image, whilst four millions of her children still abide in growing happiness under her maternal care. Verily, it was the spirit of prophecy which said, two hundred years ago, "*God will bless that ground*."

That blessing we have lived to see. May it continue for yet many centennials, and grow as it endures! May the faith and spirit of the men through whose piety and wisdom it has come still warm and animate the hearts of their successors to the latest generations! May no careless or corrupt administration of justice or "looseness" or infidelities of the people come in to bring down the wrath of Heaven for its interruption! May the sterling principles of our happy freedom be made good to us and our posterity by the good keeping of them in honest virtue and obedience, and in due reverence of Him who gave them, and who is the God and Judge of nations! May those sacred conditions of the divine favor "which descend not with worldly inheritances" be so embedded in the training and education of our youth that the spirit of the children may not be a libel on the faith and devotion of their fathers!

Centuries have passed, but the God of Gustavus Adolphus, of the Pilgrims of Plymouth Rock, of William Penn, and of the hero-saints of every age and country still lives and reigns. Men may deny it, but that does not alter it. His government and Gospel are the same now that they have ever been. What he most approved and blessed in their days he most approves and blesses in ours. And may their fear and love of him be to us and our children a copy and a guide, to steer in safety amid the dangerous rapids of these doubtful times!

"And thou, Philadelphia, the virgin settlement of this province, named before thou wert born! what love, what care, what service, and what travail has there been to bring thee forth and preserve thee from such as would abuse and defile thee! My soul prays to God for thee, that thou mayest stand in the day of trial, that thy children may be blessed of the Lord, and thy people saved by his power."

The Codes Of Hammurabi And Moses
W. W. Davies

QTY

The discovery of the Hammurabi Code is one of the greatest achievements of archaeology, and is of paramount interest, not only to the student of the Bible, but also to all those interested in ancient history...

Religion   **ISBN:** *1-59462-338-4*   **Pages:132**
MSRP $12.95

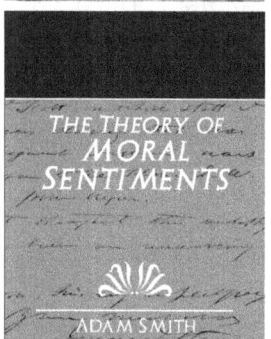

The Theory of Moral Sentiments
Adam Smith

QTY

This work from 1749. contains original theories of conscience amd moral judgment and it is the foundation for systemof morals.

Philosophy **ISBN:** *1-59462-777-0*   **Pages:536**
MSRP $19.95

Jessica's First Prayer
Hesba Stretton

QTY

In a screened and secluded corner of one of the many railway-bridges which span the streets of London there could be seen a few years ago, from five o'clock every morning until half past eight, a tidily set-out coffee-stall, consisting of a trestle and board, upon which stood two large tin cans, with a small fire of charcoal burning under each so as to keep the coffee boiling during the early hours of the morning when the work-people were thronging into the city on their way to their daily toil...

Childrens   **ISBN:** *1-59462-373-2*

Pages:84
MSRP $9.95

My Life and Work
Henry Ford

QTY

Henry Ford revolutionized the world with his implementation of mass production for the Model T automobile. Gain valuable business insight into his life and work with his own auto-biography... "We have only started on our development of our country we have not as yet, with all our talk of wonderful progress, done more than scratch the surface. The progress has been wonderful enough but..."

Pages:300

Biographies/   **ISBN:** *1-59462-198-5*   *MSRP $21.95*

The Art of Cross-Examination
Francis Wellman

QTY

I presume it is the experience of every author, after his first book is published upon an important subject, to be almost overwhelmed with a wealth of ideas and illustrations which could readily have been included in his book, and which to his own mind, at least, seem to make a second edition inevitable. Such certainly was the case with me; and when the first edition had reached its sixth impression in five months, I rejoiced to learn that it seemed to my publishers that the book had met with a sufficiently favorable reception to justify a second and considerably enlarged edition. ...

Pages:412

Reference ISBN: *1-59462-647-2*   *MSRP $19.95*

On the Duty of Civil Disobedience
Henry David Thoreau

QTY

Thoreau wrote his famous essay, On the Duty of Civil Disobedience, as a protest against an unjust but popular war and the immoral but popular institution of slave-owning. He did more than write—he declined to pay his taxes, and was hauled off to gaol in consequence. Who can say how much this refusal of his hastened the end of the war and of slavery ?

Law   ISBN: *1-59462-747-9*

Pages:48

MSRP $7.45

Dream Psychology Psychoanalysis for Beginners
Sigmund Freud

QTY

Sigmund Freud, born Sigismund Schlomo Freud (May 6, 1856 - September 23, 1939), was a Jewish-Austrian neurologist and psychiatrist who co-founded the psychoanalytic school of psychology. Freud is best known for his theories of the unconscious mind, especially involving the mechanism of repression; his redefinition of sexual desire as mobile and directed towards a wide variety of objects; and his therapeutic techniques, especially his understanding of transference in the therapeutic relationship and the presumed value of dreams as sources of insight into unconscious desires.

Pages:196

Psychology   ISBN: *1-59462-905-6*   *MSRP $15.45*

The Miracle of Right Thought
Orison Swett Marden

QTY

Believe with all of your heart that you will do what you were made to do. When the mind has once formed the habit of holding cheerful, happy, prosperous pictures, it will not be easy to form the opposite habit. It does not matter how improbable or how far away this realization may see, or how dark the prospects may be, if we visualize them as best we can, as vividly as possible, hold tenaciously to them and vigorously struggle to attain them, they will gradually become actualized, realized in the life. But a desire, a longing without endeavor, a yearning abandoned or held indifferently will vanish without realization.

Pages:360

Self Help   ISBN: *1-59462-644-8*   *MSRP $25.45*

QTY

The Rosicrucian Cosmo-Conception Mystic Christianity *by Max Heindel*   ISBN: *1-59462-188-8*   **$38.95**
The Rosicrucian Cosmo-conception is not dogmatic, neither does it appeal to any other authority than the reason of the student. It is: not controversial, but is: sent forth in the, hope that it may help to clear...   *New Age/Religion Pages 646*

Abandonment To Divine Providence *by Jean-Pierre de Caussade*   ISBN: *1-59462-228-0*   **$25.95**
"The Rev. Jean Pierre de Caussade was one of the most remarkable spiritual writers of the Society of Jesus in France in the 18th Century. His death took place at Toulouse in 1751. His works have gone through many editions and have been republished...   *Inspirational/Religion Pages 400*

Mental Chemistry *by Charles Haanel*   ISBN: *1-59462-192-6*   **$23.95**
Mental Chemistry allows the change of material conditions by combining and appropriately utilizing the power of the mind. Much like applied chemistry creates something new and unique out of careful combinations of chemicals the mastery of mental chemistry...   *New Age Pages 354*

The Letters of Robert Browning and Elizabeth Barret Barrett 1845-1846 vol II   ISBN: *1-59462-193-4*   **$35.95**
by Robert Browning and Elizabeth Barrett   *Biographies Pages 596*

Gleanings In Genesis (volume I) *by Arthur W. Pink*   ISBN: *1-59462-130-6*   **$27.45**
Appropriately has Genesis been termed "the seed plot of the Bible" for in it we have, in germ form, almost all of the great doctrines which are afterwards fully developed in the books of Scripture which follow...   *Religion/Inspirational Pages 420*

The Master Key *by L. W. de Laurence*   ISBN: *1-59462-001-6*   **$30.95**
In no branch of human knowledge has there been a more lively increase of the spirit of research during the past few years than in the study of Psychology, Concentration and Mental Discipline. The requests for authentic lessons in Thought Control, Mental Discipline and...   *New Age/Business Pages 422*

The Lesser Key Of Solomon Goetia *by L. W. de Laurence*   ISBN: *1-59462-092-X*   **$9.95**
This translation of the first book of the "Lernegton" which is now for the first time made accessible to students of Talismanic Magic was done, after careful collation and edition, from numerous Ancient Manuscripts in Hebrew, Latin, and French...   *New Age/Occult Pages 92*

Rubaiyat Of Omar Khayyam *by Edward Fitzgerald*   ISBN:*1-59462-332-5*   **$13.95**
Edward Fitzgerald, whom the world has already learned, in spite of his own efforts to remain within the shadow of anonymity, to look upon as one of the rarest poets of the century, was born at Bredfield, in Suffolk, on the 31st of March, 1809. He was the third son of John Purcell...   *Music Pages 172*

Ancient Law *by Henry Maine*   ISBN: *1-59462-128-4*   **$29.95**
The chief object of the following pages is to indicate some of the earliest ideas of mankind, as they are reflected in Ancient Law, and to point out the relation of those ideas to modern thought.   *Religiom/History Pages 452*

Far-Away Stories *by William J. Locke*   ISBN: *1-59462-129-2*   **$19.45**
"Good wine needs no bush, but a collection of mixed vintages does. And this book is just such a collection. Some of the stories I do not want to remain buried for ever in the museum files of dead magazine-numbers an author's not unpardonable vanity..."   *Fiction Pages 272*

Life of David Crockett *by David Crockett*   ISBN: *1-59462-250-7*   **$27.45**
"Colonel David Crockett was one of the most remarkable men of the times in which he lived. Born in humble life, but gifted with a strong will, an indomitable courage, and unremitting perseverance...   *Biographies/New Age Pages 424*

Lip-Reading *by Edward Nitchie*   ISBN: *1-59462-206-X*   **$25.95**
Edward B. Nitchie, founder of the New York School for the Hard of Hearing, now the Nitchie School of Lip-Reading, Inc, wrote "LIP-READING Principles and Practice". The development and perfecting of this meritorious work on lip-reading was an undertaking...   *How-to Pages 400*

A Handbook of Suggestive Therapeutics, Applied Hypnotism, Psychic Science   ISBN: *1-59462-214-0*   **$24.95**
by Henry Munro   *Health/New Age/Health/Self-help Pages 376*

A Doll's House: and Two Other Plays *by Henrik Ibsen*   ISBN: *1-59462-112-8*   **$19.95**
Henrik Ibsen created this classic when in revolutionary 1848 Rome. Introducing some striking concepts in playwriting for the realist genre, this play has been studied the world over.   *Fiction/Classics/Plays 308*

The Light of Asia *by sir Edwin Arnold*   ISBN: *1-59462-204-3*   **$13.95**
In this poetic masterpiece, Edwin Arnold describes the life and teachings of Buddha. The man who was to become known as Buddha to the world was born as Prince Gautama of India but he rejected the worldly riches and abandoned the reigns of power when...   *Religion/History/Biographies Pages 170*

The Complete Works of Guy de Maupassant *by Guy de Maupassant*   ISBN: *1-59462-157-8*   **$16.95**
"For days and days, nights and nights, I had dreamed of that first kiss which was to consecrate our engagement, and I knew not on what spot I should put my lips..."   *Fiction/Classics Pages 240*

The Art of Cross-Examination *by Francis L. Wellman*   ISBN: *1-59462-309-0*   **$26.95**
Written by a renowned trial lawyer, Wellman imparts his experience and uses case studies to explain how to use psychology to extract desired information through questioning.   *How-to/Science/Reference Pages 408*

Answered or Unanswered? *by Louisa Vaughan*   ISBN: *1-59462-248-5*   **$10.95**
Miracles of Faith in China   *Religion Pages 112*

The Edinburgh Lectures on Mental Science (1909) *by Thomas*   ISBN: *1-59462-008-3*   **$11.95**
This book contains the substance of a course of lectures recently given by the writer in the Queen Street Hall, Edinburgh. Its purpose is to indicate the Natural Principles governing the relation between Mental Action and Material Conditions...   *New Age/Psychology Pages 148*

Ayesha *by H. Rider Haggard*   ISBN: *1-59462-301-5*   **$24.95**
Verily and indeed it is the unexpected that happens! Probably if there was one person upon the earth from whom the Editor of this, and of a certain previous history, did not expect to hear again...   *Classics Pages 380*

Ayala's Angel *by Anthony Trollope*   ISBN: *1-59462-352-X*   **$29.95**
The two girls were both pretty, but Lucy who was twenty-one who supposed to be simple and comparatively unattractive, whereas Ayala was credited, as her Bombwhat romantic name might show, with poetic charm and a taste for romance. Ayala when her father died was nineteen...   *Fiction Pages 484*

The American Commonwealth *by James Bryce*   ISBN: *1-59462-286-8*   **$34.45**
An interpretation of American democratic political theory. It examines political mechanics and society from the perspective of Scotsman James Bryce   *Politics Pages 572*

Stories of the Pilgrims *by Margaret P. Pumphrey*   ISBN: *1-59462-116-0*   **$17.95**
This book explores pilgrims religious oppression in England as well as their escape to Holland and eventual crossing to America on the Mayflower, and their early days in New England...   *History Pages 268*

www.bookjungle.com *email: sales@bookjungle.com fax: 630-214-0564 mail: Book Jungle PO Box 2226 Champaign, IL 61825*

QTY

The Fasting Cure *by Sinclair Upton*   ISBN: *1-59462-222-1* **$13.95**
In the Cosmopolitan Magazine for May, 1910, and in the Contemporary Review (London) for April, 1910, I published an article dealing with my experiences in fasting. I have written a great many magazine articles, but never one which attracted so much attention... New Age/Self Help/Health Pages 164

Hebrew Astrology *by Sepharial*   ISBN: *1-59462-308-2* **$13.45**
In these days of advanced thinking it is a matter of common observation that we have left many of the old landmarks behind and that we are now pressing forward to greater heights and to a wider horizon than that which represented the mind-content of our progenitors... Astrology Pages 144

Thought Vibration or The Law of Attraction in the Thought World   ISBN: *1-59462-127-6* **$12.95**

by William Walker Atkinson   *Psychology/Religion Pages 144*

Optimism *by Helen Keller*   ISBN: *1-59462-108-X* **$15.95**
Helen Keller was blind, deaf, and mute since 19 months old, yet famously learned how to overcome these handicaps, communicate with the world, and spread her lectures promoting optimism. An inspiring read for everyone... Biographies/Inspirational Pages 84

Sara Crewe *by Frances Burnett*   ISBN: *1-59462-360-0* **$9.45**
In the first place, Miss Minchin lived in London. Her home was a large, dull, tall one, in a large, dull square, where all the houses were alike, and all the sparrows were alike, and where all the door-knockers made the same heavy sound... Childrens/Classic Pages 88

The Autobiography of Benjamin Franklin *by Benjamin Franklin*   ISBN: *1-59462-135-7* **$24.95**
The Autobiography of Benjamin Franklin has probably been more extensively read than any other American historical work, and no other book of its kind has had such ups and downs of fortune. Franklin lived for many years in England, where he was agent... Biographies History Pages 332

Name

Email

Telephone

Address

City, State ZIP

☐ Credit Card   ☐ Check / Money Order

Credit Card Number

Expiration Date

Signature

Please Mail to: Book Jungle
PO Box 2226
Champaign, IL 61825
or Fax to: 630-214-0564

ORDERING INFORMATION
web*: www.bookjungle.com*
email*: sales@bookjungle.com*
fax*: 630-214-0564*
mail*: Book Jungle PO Box 2226 Champaign, IL 61825*
or PayPal *to sales@bookjungle.com*

Please contact us for bulk discounts

DIRECT-ORDER TERMS

20% Discount if You Order Two or More Books
Free Domestic Shipping!
Accepted: Master Card, Visa, Discover, American Express

www.ingramcontent.com/pod-product-compliance
Lightning Source LLC
Chambersburg PA
CBHW082014170626
46817CB00009B/3091